SUSAN INTERFERES

SUSAN INTERFERES

by

JANE SHAW

THE CHILDREN'S PRESS
LONDON AND GLASGOW

This Impression 1966

FOR
MARY AND KATH

PRINTED IN GREAT BRITAIN

CONTENTS

CHAPTER ONE

THE CARMICHAEL family and Susan bundled out of the high Swiss train on to the station platform at Lucerne. Dr. Carmichael threw out luggage, Aunt Lucy looked round for a porter and said in a desperate voice, "We'll miss the last boat to Rosendorf! It leaves at seven o'clock! We'll never get it! If we could only find a porter——!"

Susan, in her helpful way, bumbled along the platform and accosted a strong-looking man in uniform. As he was a high-ranking officer in the Swiss army he didn't take too kindly to the idea of portering the Carmichaels' luggage. Blushing slightly, Susan returned to the others and found that a porter had been secured and was piling the luggage on to a barrow. When Aunt Lucy said "Rosendorf," in an anxious voice, the porter became excited too and began to push his barrow along the platform at a shambling trot. He waved vaguely to the right. "Go to the boat," he said, "and I will bring the luggage."

Aunt Lucy didn't really want to lose sight of either the porter or the luggage, but the whole family was running through the station now in the direction of a large notice which announced BOATS in three languages, so she ran with them. Susan stopped to help an elderly woman who was lugging her heavy case along the platform with obvious difficulty; but her motives were misunderstood, the elderly woman clung madly to her case and when Susan, determined to help her, laid hands on the case, she was greeted with shrill remonstrances in a very foreign language.

Midge glanced back over her shoulder and called, "Oh *do* stop interfering, Susie, and come *on*! We don't want to miss the boat——"

"She thought I was trying to steal her bag," Susan kindly explained, as she and Midge hurried after the others.

Midge didn't reply. She didn't much care for running at the best of times; laden with coats and cameras and raincoats and a parcel of Aunt Lucy's in a foreign town at seven o'clock on a warm evening she cared for it even less and wasn't going to waste any of her precious breath telling Susan what she thought of her.

The boat—a little trim single-decker motor-boat called the *Mythen*—was fortunately still at the quay. Susan and the Carmichaels flung themselves on, the porter flung their luggage on, and as they looked at each other beaming delightedly at having caught the boat, all the bells in Lucerne began to ring.

"Oh, how *lovely*," cried Susan, "just as if they were ringing for us!"

Aunt Lucy counted heads and luggage. Susan helped her, and counted Bill twice and alarmed Aunt Lucy considerably, for an extra one collected in their wild dash for the boat was a worrying thought.

"Well, I'm sorry!" said Susan. "It's all this excitement! Being Abroad!"

It was something to be excited about. None of them, not even Charlotte who was nearly seventeen, had ever been abroad before. Aunt Lucy had, of course, and Uncle Charles, but not for simply ages, and here they were now, actually on a steamer on Lake Lucerne!

Susan's name was Susan Lyle, she was Scots, and while her parents were in Africa she was living with Uncle Charles and her cousins the Carmichaels—Charlotte, Midge, who was about Susan's own age which was fourteen, and Bill who was only eleven and jolly lucky to be going abroad at his age, as Midge hadn't failed to point out when she wanted to be aggravating. Aunt Lucy was their aunt too, she was Uncle Charles's sister and she had looked after them ever since their mother had died when Bill was quite small.

Bill hung over the side of the boat, watching the swans, their black feet clear in the green water, rocking on the waves as the little boat fussed away from the quay. The others settled themselves in a little nook sheltered from the breeze which blew cold now across the lake.

Midge said, "There's one thing I'm disappointed about——"

"*Disappointed?*" interrupted Susan, waving a hand round—at Lucerne behind them, guarded by the handsome bulk of Mount Pilatus, and before them the smooth waters of the lake and fold upon fold of mountains, snow-capped, dim and mysterious in the evening light.

"I *had* thought," Midge went on, "that in Switzerland we'd have been spared Susan rushing about helping and rescuing people and generally interfering with their lives——"

"Why?" asked Susan. She had had—before the unfortunate episodes in the station—a good deal of success recently in her rescuing and helping and interfering and poking her nose generally into other people's business. "Why?" she said.

"Well," said Midge, "the language. German or Swiss or *Schwyzerdütsch* or whatever they call it. You can't speak a word. I must say I thought that would cramp you a bit. And yet the minute you set foot on Swiss soil you start trying to carry an old lady's bag for her——"

Susan giggled. "That wasn't one of my more successful efforts," she admitted. "Silly old thing thought I was trying to steal her blessed bag. She spoke some perfectly frightful language—goodness, I *was* silly, I should have tried French! I can speak French. *Je me promène. Je fais un petit tour en ville*," she said, just to prove it. "People in Switzerland speak French, don't they, Aunt Lucy?"

Aunt Lucy tore her attention away from the contemplation of the little villages on the lake-shores, the wooded slopes and the high mountains, grim and forbidding now as the darkness gathered. "Some do," she said. "But not in this part of Switzerland."

"I expect they can all speak a bit of French even in the German-speaking part," said Susan confidently.

"All the same," Midge said, "I don't see that being able to say *I go for a walk, I take a little turn through the town* gives you much scope. Luckily."

"Besides," said Susan, ignoring Midge, "some of them can speak English. That porter could. And look at Fräulein Amacher!"

This Fräulein Amacher had been the go-between in the correspondence between Aunt Lucy, who didn't know enough German to write letters, and the proprietor of the hotel where they were going to stay, who didn't know enough English. Aunt Lucy had picked the little hotel on the shores of Lake Lucerne from the innumerable leaflets collected from the travel agencies, and when she had written asking for rooms, this Fräulein Amacher had replied.

"Oh, Fräulein Amacher!" said Aunt Lucy. "I feel that she's quite a friend already after all those complicated letters that we exchanged."

Susan gazed over the waters of the lake and said musingly for about the twentieth time. "I can't think why she wanted us to bring a pound of tea with us——"

"She told us why," said Midge, also for the twentieth time. "Fräulein Amacher loves real English tea and it is expensive here——"

Aunt Lucy suddenly clutched Susan's arm. "Have you got the parcel?" she said.

"I haven't got it," said Susan blankly, and darting to the luggage began to hunt frantically.

"I've got it," Midge said calmly. "Susan does all the talking while I do the actual carrying."

She glanced down at the parcel on her knee—a funny little man had brought it to the house two days before.

Susan looked down at the parcel too. "I can't believe that's the real reason Fräulein Amacher asked us to bring it," she said. "I mean because it's expensive. You can't tell me that anyone would ask us to cart a pound of tea halfway across Europe just because it's expensive here. Surely no one could care all that about *tea*? Goodness, *I* wouldn't care if I never tasted tea again in the whole of my life!"

Susan had had in the back of her mind that the Swiss customs would rip open the parcel of tea and that out would come tumbling a whole stream of illicit diamonds or dollars or some such thing. Nothing like that had happened. Aunt Lucy had said in a casual voice that she had some tea for a friend and the customs man hadn't even glanced at the parcel—or any of their luggage for that matter, only made his little chalk mark on the cases and the customs' examination was over. It was very disappointing. Of course, Susan had thought, it would have been pretty awful if diamonds *had* come pouring out and a terrible disgrace, right there in front of everybody, but on the other hand she just couldn't believe that there was only tea in the parcel. She had been longing to open it ever since the odd little man, with the broken accent and the sad and anxious eyes, had brought it to the house. She felt like Bluebeard's wife who couldn't rest until she had seen inside the forbidden room. She fingered the parcel now, prodding it, poking at a corner—it certainly felt like tea——

"Susan, do leave that parcel alone," said Aunt Lucy. "You'll burst the wrapping-paper and then where shall we be? Tea all over the boat—and it's so clean too——"

"There must be something else behind it," said Susan. "I wonder what it can be? Of course I can ask Fräulein Amacher as soon as we get there——"

"Oh help," said Midge. "Starting your interfering early."

The boat called at little villages and Susan and the Carmichaels hung over the side and gazed at the trim piers and the pretty hotels and the chalets with their window-boxes full of geraniums and petunias. The lake became narrower and the mountains steeper and wilder and more awesome in the twilight. And then, as the lights began to gleam on the edge of the lake, they were at Rosendorf, and they staggered ashore with their luggage, Susan trying to carry everyone else's share as well as her own and causing such confusion that everybody really was thankful to pick out the round-faced smiling porter, with *Chalet du Lac* on his cap, from the waiting row of porters. He pointed along the lake-side to some coloured, twinking lights; that was the Chalet du Lac, he said, and piled the luggage into a little trailer behind his bicycle. Bill was dying to ride in the trailer too, but the porter didn't encourage this idea so they all walked through the village towards the hotel. Aunt Lucy cast a longing eye at a shop that was simply bursting with Swiss things—wood carvings and brooches like flowers and embroideries—but, she said, she was so desperate with hunger that she couldn't stop even to glance at all those tempting things, and Bill said he should think *not*.

The hotel was about five minutes' walk from the pier; it was almost on the lake, with the garden between it and the water and a terrace built right on the water's edge with tables and chairs. The Carmichaels' rooms were in a chalet in the garden, a real old chalet of dark-brown wood, with tremendous wide eaves; a double flight of steps led up to the front door, and there were flowers everywhere, geraniums and petunias on every step and on the little balconies. Even an old water trough in the garden, hollowed out of a log, was smothered in geraniums. Each room had a veranda, Aunt Lucy and Caroline had rooms that looked over to Mount Pilatus, Susan and Midge shared a room looking up the lake where already the lights of other villages twinkled along the fringe of the water and far up the mountains. Bill and Uncle Charles had a view over the lake too, but Bill said that he really didn't know in which direction, because just at the moment the only view he wanted to look at was a view of the dinner-table. The linen on the beds was snowy-white and there were enormous great white billowing sort of eiderdowns on each bed. Aunt Lucy dredged her memory and said that she thought they were called *duvets*, and that although they looked rather fun they were really frightful because if you kept them on you were apt to die of prickly heat, and if you didn't, you died of cold.

The dining-room had huge windows wide open to the warm evening and window-boxes filled with nasturtiums, and their table was right by the window. They had a heavenly dinner—soup and mounds of roast veal in the biggest dish they had ever seen and lots of different vegetables and a green salad and caramel cream for pudding, and after they had finished they put their table-napkins into little envelopes on which they all wrote their names.

After dinner Aunt Lucy muttered something about bed, but everybody quite rightly ignored this senseless remark, and they all went for a walk through the village. And all the shops were open—"Fancy!" said Susan. "At this time of night!"—half their wares displayed outside and swarms of visitors were hanging round the little carvings and the pretty brooches, the cuckoo-clocks, the cuckoo-whistles and the rows and rows of postcards, and Charlotte said that Switzerland was the first place that she had ever seen that really was like the picture postcards, only better. Then they sat down at a café. It was called the Confiserie Hofmann and it was lit with soft hidden coloured lights and a tiny orchestra was playing and people were dancing. But the Carmichaels sat at a table on the pavement and had coffee and ices and the most luscious cakes and Aunt Lucy said honestly, she didn't know where they put it, after that enormous dinner, and Susan looked through the trees towards the lake, where the lights of Rosendorf were reflected in the smooth water, and to the other lights twinkling in the mountains halfway up to the sky, and sighed. "Och," she said, "and to think that it's all going to be spoiled!"

"Three guesses as to what's going to spoil it," muttered Midge.

"We only need one," said Charlotte.

"The ghastly Gascoignes!" said Bill and made loud and dramatic groaning noises.

"Nonsense," said Aunt Lucy automatically. She was still vainly hoping that if she told her family often enough how delightful, original, talented and charming the Gascoignes were that they would come in the end to believe her. "You'll enjoy their company——"

"Like we'd enjoy the company of a family of poisonous snakes," said Midge.

Dr. Carmichael, far from his patients and night-calls and the ever-ringing telephone and loving it, as he sat back watching the summer crowds strolling by, at peace with all the world, said, "I thought you liked the Gascoignes. Charming little woman, Mrs. Gascoigne——"

The Carmichaels and Susan glanced at each other. A few short days before such a remark would have plunged them in despair because they had feared that their father was going to marry the widowed Mrs. Gascoigne; instead she had got herself engaged to somebody else, and the very recollection of the fate that they had escaped, made them feel—if only temporarily—more benevolent towards the whole family.[1]

"Adrian's not so bad, is he, Charlotte?" said Midge. Charlotte blushed slightly but said nothing.

"I *suppose*," said Susan in a doubtful voice, "that if

[1] See *Susan Rushes In*

Gabrielle cleaned herself up a bit and stopped wearing her hair in that ghastly horse's-tail and stopped being so stuck-up and conceited she would be more or less all right—improved, at least——"

"Nothing," said Bill gloomily, "would improve that Pea-green except dropping him from an aeroplane at the height of—say—ten thousand feet——"

"Still," said Midge, glancing at Charlotte again, "Adrian's not so bad, is he, Charlotte? Just as long as we don't have him in the family——"

Charlotte, goaded, burst out, "Just because he happened to ask me out once or twice doesn't mean he's going to be in the family!"

Midge, having got the desired rise out of Charlotte, grinned at her happily. Charlotte made a face at her, then unwillingly grinned back.

"I expect he'll take you dancing at that grand hotel they're going to," said Susan. "You can tell us what it's like inside——"

"That's one good thing," said Midge, "that they're going to a different hotel——"

"And don't forget that we have nearly two weeks before they come," said Susan, who usually looked on the bright side of things.

"And perhaps," said Bill, trying to smother a yawn, "perhaps we shan't be bothered with them too much after all——"

But Aunt Lucy had seen the yawn. She glanced at her watch and gave a little shriek. "Bill! It's ten o'clock! You should have been in bed hours ago! And after all that travelling to-day too! Come along everybody—*bed*!"

So they went slowly and reluctantly back along the lake-side to the Chalet du Lac, the warm air soft against their faces, the water lapping gently against the stones, the lights on the lake a faint shimmer.

CHAPTER TWO

Up the Airy Mountains

SUSAN AWOKE to a twittering of birds. She opened sleepy eyes and saw two sparrows having a violent argument on the rail of her balcony and making enough noise, she considered, for a couple of swans. Susan crawled out from under her *duvet* and stood at the window, shivering slightly in the cool air of morning. The lake looked cold and grey, the ranks of snow-peaks cold too, austere and forbidding. Then suddenly it happened—the still-hidden sun caught the high mountains and the topmost peaks became flushed with pink. Susan was enchanted. She was about to waken Midge to show her this wonder when she remembered that Midge would be as mad as a snake to be roused at that hour in the morning even for the glories of the sunrise, so she slipped back into bed and sat with her arms round her knees and watched the distant mountain tops until the pink faded, even from the lowest snow slopes and from the twin peaks, two distant triangles of snow just appearing beyond the bulk of the dark, nearer mountains. Her peaks, Susan felt they were, her special little twin-peaks, she thought sleepily as she wriggled under the sheets again. In the distance she heard a sweet, flat tinkle. Gosh! she thought, drifting off to sleep, cowbells! Gosh, I really am in Switzerland! I must tell Midge. . . .

When next she woke, the sun was streaming in the window, swallows were swooping over the lake in mad exuberance and the first steamer of the day was announcing its approach to the pier by giving a peremptory toot outside Susan's bedroom window. She leapt out of bed and grabbed her camera and quickly took a photo of the trim little ship. Then she set herself to the monumental task of rousing Midge and persuading her into the lake for a swim.

When Susan and Midge eventually made their way to the dining-room, they found the rest of the family seated at the table by the huge open windows. To their annoyance Charlotte and Bill had bagged the window seats, but Aunt Lucy said peaceably that they needn't start arguing, that everybody would take turns in sitting at the window. Bill was staring at a plate of hot rolls and *croissants* and things called *swieback* (which turned out to be a kind of thin sweet rusk, done up in packets) and a pot of steaming coffee— for Aunt Lucy and Dr. Carmichael, and a pot of steaming chocolate—for himself and Charlotte. He whispered anxiously, "Is this all?"

Aunt Lucy said that it was, that this was the Continental breakfast.

"No bacon and eggs?"

"No."

"No scrambled eggs?"

"No."

"Not even boiled eggs?"

"No."

"Oh crumbs," said Bill.

A cheerful little fair-haired waitress in a snowy embroidered apron brought more rolls and jam and chocolate for Midge and Susan and beamed at them all. "You go a little bit on top of a mountain to-day, yes?" she asked.

Yes, Aunt Lucy thought, the sooner they got up among those mountains, the better and a packed lunch for six was being ordered when Aunt Lucy, to everybody's intense astonishment, was called to the telephone.

"Who on *earth* can want Aunt Lucy on the telephone?" said Charlotte.

"Who knows she's here?" said Midge.

"How will she manage to speak on a Swiss telephone?" asked Bill.

"Don't you think I'd better go and help her?" said Susan in her interfering way. "In case she does get into difficulties with the language?"

Everybody burst into jeering laughter at this suggestion, and in the middle of it Aunt Lucy came back and announced that her call was from Fräulein Amacher, who had asked them all to tea next day.

They all looked a bit doubtful at that, as Susan and her cousins wondered if going to tea with a strange Swiss lady was a good way to spend one of their precious afternoons.

"Are you sure that's what she said?" asked Susan. "Perhaps you didn't understand her properly, Aunt Lucy, talking Swiss or whatever she was talking— Perhaps she was asking about her pound of tea——?"

"Fräulein Amacher speaks perfect English," Aunt Lucy said. So that was more reassuring, and they decided to explore Lucerne the next day, finishing up at Fräulein Amacher's for tea, as it was in Lucerne that Fräulein Amacher lived.

"And now what about this mountain?" said Uncle Charles, who had finished his coffee and rolls long ago and was itching to be on the move. "Shall we go up the Rigi?"

"Go up the Rigi," said Midge in a faint voice. "The Rigi is a huge mountain! Thousands of feet high!"

"Almost six thousand, to be exact," said Bill, who had been consulting a pamphlet about excursions from Rosendorf which he had collected from the reception desk before breakfast.

"Six thousand feet!" exclaimed Midge. "I couldn't climb up six thousand feet! I'd drop dead on the way! Probably after six *hundred*——"

Uncle Charles laughed. "Nobody asked you to climb up six thousand feet," he said. "Not that it would do you any harm, you lazy little monkey. No, we go up the Rigi in a train——"

"In a train!" said Midge.

"Yes, didn't you know? There are mountain railways up lots of these Swiss mountains——"

"Oh well then," said Midge. Going up in a train was exactly her idea of mountain-climbing.

"And we'll walk down," said Aunt Lucy enthusiastically.

"Aunt Lucy!" said Midge, faint again. "Must you ruin the whole day?"

"Och away, Midge," said Susan. "Coming down will be *nothing*, just a wee stroll——"

Bill undertook to look up a suitable boat in the

time-table in the hall and Aunt Lucy undertook to get them all along to the pier in time for it. In the morning sunshine, Rosendorf was bright and clean and gay; the little shops had their wares already spread out on trestle tables on the pavement: not a ripple crept over the lake and the mountains were wreathed in a haze of heat. Everywhere there were flowers—there were flowers at the windows of the hotels, of the village school, of the little old brown chalets, of the pretty new villas, there were geraniums in a tiny window half-hidden under a flight of steps leading higher up the village. In the gardens, called the Kurplatz, beside the lake there were roses—even climbing up the lamp standards and over the little bandstand. "No wonder they call this place Rosendorf," said Aunt Lucy as they panted towards the pier laden with macs, cardigans, cameras and packets of lunch done up in very pretty paper carriers with pictures of Swiss flowers on them. "Roses everywhere."

"Does Rosendorf mean roses, then?" asked Susan.

"It means little town of roses, I *think*," said Aunt Lucy.

It was a bigger boat than the one which had brought them from Lucerne the previous night, called the *Gallia*. Bill wrote its name down in his diary—he was making a list, he said, of all the boats on the lake. It was packed with people, all beaming happily, all carrying rucksacks or packets of lunch and walking-sticks and many were wearing huge climbing-boots. The sight of them, Midge said, made her feel tired and slightly faint.

Susan and the Carmichaels said what fun it was going everywhere by boat, *much* nicer than trains or buses or even luxurious limousines; and they leant over the side and admired Rosendorf from this new angle. The Chalet du Lac, said Susan, looked easily the nicest hotel—the new bit very smart and trim and their own little chalet sweet and pretty and smothered in flowers. It was almost the last house in the village, except for one, a beautiful chalet, big and old and rambling, set in beautiful gardens that glowed with flowers.

They left the boat at a place called Vitznau, and most of the boat-load left with them. Just a step from the pier, almost in the middle of the village street, a little red train was waiting. Everybody bundled into this, except the stalwart spirits in the climbing-boots, and off they went, practically straight up in the air, Susan felt, creeping up the side of the mountain; and in a minute they were looking down on the red roofs of Vitznau, and in another minute the lake was spreading out below them as they saw farther and farther into its blue distances, and hitherto unrevealed snow peaks appeared above and beyond the mountains they had seen from below.

Bill read them little bits out of the guide-books and pamphlets with which he had provided himself. He seemed determined to improve their minds, but as the others did not seem much in the mood to have their minds improved the conversation was slightly disjointed.

"It says here," he said, "that this was the first mountain railway in Europe——"

"Oh the flowers! The fields are full of flowers!"

"I can see Rosendorf—look there's the Chalet, just a dot!"

"I think I'll take up flower painting——"

"It's a pity the mountains are so hazy——"

"What's happening to my ears? They're going snap, crackle, pop, like in the aeroplane!"

"Oh Susan it's the altitude—wait, I have some sweets somewhere for you to suck——"

"It says here that the railway used to be steam——"

"Oh thank you, Aunt Lucy——"

"Keep sucking hard and swallowing—is that better?"

"I don't know if it's any better but it's much nicer—I'm enjoying the sweetie——"

"It says here that the railway was first built in 1871——"

"Help! 1871! That's *ancient*!" said Susan, taking notice of Bill's information at last. "D'you think it's safe?"

"Oh, don't be dotty, Susie, it has been all done up since then. It was electrified in 1937——"

"Look at the cows! Aren't they a nice colour? Sort of fawn——"

"They've got *huge* bells round their necks, some of them——"

"Oh, look at these blue flowers—can they be gentians?"

"How queer, these chalets are lying on their backs!"

"Don't be dotty, Susie, that's you, not the chalets——"

"*I'm* not lying on my back!"

"No, of course not, it's the angle of the train——"

"They've got massive great stones on the roofs——"

"That's to stop the roofs falling off——"

"And look at the wood and logs stacked up at the sides under the eaves—how neat!"

"Oh, we're stopping—are we there?"

The little red train stopped once or twice at tiny wayside stations, where there were only a few chalets and a hotel, and Susan in her eagerness had to be restrained from getting out at each one. But after about half an hour the train reached Rigi Kulm and everybody got out. As they alighted they hastily pulled on jerseys and pullovers, for a thick mist was everywhere and it was suddenly bitterly cold. "There's a hotel," said Uncle Charles, "what about some coffee to heat us up?" Everybody thought that this was a good idea, and they had coffee and Susan sent a post-card to her mother and father in Africa with *Rigi Kulm*, 1800 *mètres* stamped on it, which, she said, didn't sound nearly so high as 6,000 feet.

She also bought some edelweiss in a little packet. "I'd rather have found it," she said, looking at the strange thick white flowers which she thought looked rather like flannel only she didn't like to say so, "somehow to buy it doesn't seem quite the thing, like buying white heather instead of finding it for yourself."

"You couldn't get it by yourself," said Bill, getting the information out of his book as usual, "edelweiss is a protected plant in Switzerland and you're not allowed to pick it even if you do find it which isn't very likely."

By that time the mist had cleared and they were able to walk about the top of the ridge of the Rigi in bright sunshine. The distant mountains, however, were still hazy and they did not get the splendid views of the mountains and the Alps of the Bernese Oberland and even the Vosges Mountains which are in France and *miles* from the Rigi which Bill's book had promised them, which was disappointing for everybody except Susan. For she had discovered as they climbed up the mountain in the little train and looked down steep slopes and precipitous ravines that she didn't really terribly like heights. She was very ashamed of this and so didn't say anything, but just agreed with everybody that it was a pity to miss the view in a very hypocritical way.

What she liked were the little shops on the very top of the Rigi. Not proper shops, but stalls laid out with the usual array of carved bears and ash-trays and musical boxes and embroidered handker-chiefs and toy chalets, with little pumps and wood stacked under the eaves and flowers in their window-boxes.

A crowd of little schoolboys swarmed up as she stood there, and gathered round the stall fingering and looking at everything, like Susan, and asking prices in Swiss. Then their schoolmaster appeared, barking orders at them and cuffing them on the side of the head when their responses weren't as speedy as he would have liked. Susan smiled at them as they crowded round her, jostling her and jogging her elbow. She turned away and lifted the lid of a musical box which had attracted her. Suddenly as the little tinkling tune began to play she felt a ringing box on the ear. She whirled round in indignation.

When the master found, not one of his erring pupils but an absolutely strange girl glaring at him, his expression was comical in its dismay. He gabbled something in Swiss, then changed immediately to rather stiff English. "Fräulein," he stammered, "a thousand, thousand apologies! I think—I think that it is one of my scholars who play the music-box after I order everyone to go——"

Susan rubbed her cheek, still red and smarting from the blow, rather annoyed at the ring of grinning faces round her. But she was not a girl who could ever harbour resentment for long, so she quite quickly smiled and said, "Oh, that's all right. It didn't hurt— much." However her sense of justice forced her to continue, "But Herr—Monsieur—er—do you think it's *right* to hit small boys on the head? My uncle— and he's a doctor and ought to know—once knew a little boy who was hit on the head and he went deaf and stayed deaf for the rest of his life. My uncle thinks that the fleshy part of the leg is the best place to hit small boys——"

The schoolmaster was looking anything but pleased at this lecture. "Fräulein," he said bowing stiffly and quite red with annoyance, "thank you for your advice. Again I highly apologise——"

He flicked his fingers furiously at his boys, who meekly filed off after him, nudging each other and giggling. One turned round and waved at Susan, grinning. Susan waved back; then looked up to find

Midge and Bill watching her and trying to keep straight faces.

"Now there's a man of sense," said Midge as Susan came up to them. "Didn't know you from Adam but realised at once that you'd be none the worse of a good slap! How right he was! What were you doing, Susie, interfering as usual?"

"I was not, then!" said Susan indignantly. "I wasn't doing a thing! I was just standing there looking at a wee musical box when suddenly I get a biff on the ear that nearly knocks me for six! He's off his rocker I should think. Going about clouting total strangers on the head! Thought I was a boy, he said!"

"I should think he must be a bit off," Bill said. "He should have known you weren't a boy. No boy would behave in the loony way you behave. Still," he hurried on as Susan opened her mouth to comment on the injustice of these remarks, "still, you got your own back, giving him all that blah about boys going deaf——"

"Well it's true!" Susan exclaimed, indignant again. "Uncle Charles told me himself! It's very wrong to hit people on the head!"

"Perhaps all those little Swiss boys will grow up to bless you and your interfering ways," said Midge. "And if they do they'll be unique——"

Susan still protested that she hadn't been interfering with anybody, that it had been an absolutely unprovoked attack, and Midge said, "Oh well, never mind, come on, we're going to have lunch now, you'll never see the dear man again, that's one consolation——" and they went off to have lunch. Susan would have been amazed if anyone had told her that she not only *would* see the hot-tempered schoolmaster again, but that she would be very glad to see him when she did.

They went down a little way off the ridge to a sunny sheltered spot that Aunt Lucy had found above the path and there they had lunch. In each packet were slices of cold veal, roll and butter, bread and butter, slices of cheese, a hard-boiled egg, a packet of biscuits, an apple and an orange and a twist of salt. They all ate everything except the salt, their appetites sharpened by the keen mountain air. Then Uncle Charles and Midge went to sleep and Charlotte sketched them, and very unbecoming sketches they made. Aunt Lucy and Bill gathered up all the picnic scraps and Susan tried to get everyone to stop what they were doing and start doing something else but she didn't get very far with this interfering as nobody paid any attention to her.

After about half an hour, however, she could not stand this inactivity any longer and started nagging everybody to get on with their walk. "There's plenty of time," said Bill calmly. "The book says that the descent takes two hours, which I reckon will be three hours at the rate we walk, and even that will get us back to the Chalet du Lac in heaps of time for dinner."

Midge stirred in her sleep. "Three hours' walking!" she murmured. "I'll die. I'm warning you——"

"Och away, Midge," said Susan. "It's downhill——"

In spite of Susan's rushing about like a sheep-dog trying to round up its errant flock, they were all on their way in five minutes, down the twisting path, by the green, flowery meadows, through the pine trees, with the distant marvellous views of the lake and the hazy mountains. The little red trains passed them once or twice and each time Midge gazed at them, sighing. They didn't hurry, but sat in the sun when they felt like it, but not as often as Midge felt like it, and stopped at a tiny village and had a look at the single shop and watched the gentle-eyed cows and exclaimed over the enormous size of the bells that some of them wore. Susan, as a matter of fact, wanted something done about that—the *least* she could do, she thought, was to complain to the farmers or the R.S.P.C.A.—or somebody. Bill said that they weren't as heavy as they looked, but Susan said that she would like to be sure of that.

They came at last to a cluster of brown chalets perched on the hillside which was the mountain village of Kaltbad. Aunt Lucy said that this name meant *cold bath* but nobody believed her. They found a dairy with a cat asleep in the window among nice old-fashioned butter moulds and churns, and the young girl who was in charge sitting on a bench in the sun knitting. Between Aunt Lucy's very halting German and Bill's sign-language they made her understand that they would like to buy some milk and she gave them cartons of ice-cold milk. Then, Susan having been restrained by force from ripping out her knitting and showing her the English way to do it, they, as they always did, looked for shops and found a very nice one packed with the usual tempting souvenirs. Aunt Lucy and the girls immediately began poring over these delightful objects and Uncle Charles and

Bill sighed and went to another shop to buy some chocolate to cheer themselves up. When they came back Bill was telling everybody that it was very difficult choosing because there were so many different varieties each one more luscious than the next, when Midge suddenly stuck her elbow in Susan's ribs and whispered, "Do you see what I see?"

"How should I know what you see, you daft scone?" Susan asked.

"Over there, right in the middle of the street, practically——"

"The train, d'you mean?"

" 'Mm. Let's take it. I've had enough walking. Goodness, this is supposed to be a holiday——"

Susan giggled. "Okay," she said.

Midge whispered something to Bill, and the two girls unobtrusively slid away and jumped into the little train just as the doors were clanged shut. Susan and Midge leaned out and waved at the others who were looking at them with startled faces. "See you at the bottom!" yelled Midge.

Bill suddenly doubled up with giggles, slapping his knees and pointing at them.

"What's so funny?" demanded Midge, turning to Susan.

Susan looked towards her relations who were now all giggling. "Oh help!" she said. "It's the train! It's going the wrong way! Hey, stop the train!"

Well of course the little red train wasn't going to stop its natural progress up to the Rigi Kulm even for Susan.

Midge settled herself as comfortably as she could

on the wooden seat and said, "Oh well, what's the difference? We just get an extra ride, that's all."

Susan wasn't so philosophical. She felt sure that by a little organising she could alter the Swiss railway system and persuade a train that was going up the mountain to turn and go down the mountain instead, but after a lot of wild talk about jumping out and pulling the communication cord, which she couldn't see anyway, she became calmer and sat down and resigned herself to admiring the scenery all over again.

It wasn't until the train reached Rigi Kulm that their true situation dawned on them. All the passengers left the train and handed their tickets to a ticket inspector. Susan and Midge looked at each other.

"We haven't got a ticket!" said Susan.

"No," Midge agreed.

"We haven't any money!" Susan's voice went up to a high squeak.

"No," said Midge.

"What are we to do?" said Susan.

"Nothing," said Midge.

"We can't just sit here doing nothing!" exclaimed Susan. "We must think of something! Look! He's coming along the platform! Duck!" Susan crouched down on the floor between the two seats and dragged a reluctant Midge after her. "We must hide!" She huddled on the floor and shut her eyes tight. "What's he doing now?" she whispered.

"How should I know?" muttered Midge. "I've got my head tucked in like an ostrich, just the same as you."

Feeling very uncomfortable, they remained on all fours until some descending passengers came on to the little train, when the girls sat up looking innocent and unconcerned. Then the train started off down the mountain and Susan and Midge admired the scenery once more.

When they were almost at Vitznau they realised that their position now wasn't any better than it had been at the top of the Rigi.

"Have you any plans about the tickets that we haven't got?" Midge asked. "Or shall one of us slip off and find the others?"

Susan stared at her blankly. "But the others aren't coming back this way!" she said. "They're walking straight back to Rosendorf! Don't you remember, Bill showed us the path on his map!"

"You don't mean it!" said Midge. "I saw Bill waving a map around but as he has been waving maps around until it felt like a geography lesson with old Smithy, naturally I didn't look. What a bore!"

Everybody streamed off the train and Midge and Susan crouched down between the seats again.

Midge said, "I'm getting a teeny bit fed up with this humble position. You're supposed to be the practical one of the family, why don't you think of a plan to get us off this train?"

"Well, I am thinking," said Susan, looking harassed.

"Take care the strain doesn't damage you for life," said Midge.

"What about you?" said Susan indignantly, "all you do is loll on the floor and it was your bright idea to take the train that got us into this mess! Why don't *you* get us out of it?"

"Quite right," Midge said. "I couldn't agree more. So let's just walk off. If the ticket-man is still there we'll explain what has happened and promise to send him the money——"

This plan sounded a bit too simple to Susan. "And what about the boat?" she said, just looking for difficulties, Midge thought.

"Oh let's get off the train first," she said. "We can worry about the boat later——"

They got up off the floor and dusted each other down, although one of the nice things about the Swiss trains was that they were so clean that even on the floor there was scarcely any dust, and as they were walking along the compartment to the door the train moved off.

"Hey!" shouted Susan. "Hey, we want to get off!"

Nobody, however, stopped the train; it just crept relentlessly up the mountainside towards the flowery meadows, leaving the roofs of Vitznau far below once more.

"Oh well," said Midge, settling herself in her corner again, "we might as well enjoy the scenery——"

When they reached the top, they automatically crouched down between the seats again. "I feel as if I'd been doing this all my life," said Midge, "like a pair of Flying Dutchmen, sort of, condemned to wander up and down for ever. Wouldn't it be awful if we really *were*——?"

"Really were what?" asked Susan. "Dutchmen?"

"No, condemned to go up and down the Rigi for ever——"

This thought made Susan rather gloomy. "Do the trains go on all night?" she asked.

"I don't know," said Midge. "We need Bill with his little book."

"We need Uncle Charles with some tickets," said Susan.

This time they hadn't long to wait in hiding. Large numbers of people were now ready to descend the mountain and were waiting for the train. Two bullet-headed small boys came into the part of the train where Midge and Susan were and came up to the end of the carriage, pushing and shoving at each other which seems to be the way that small boys normally progress. Susan and Midge quickly stopped lolling about and pretended to be very busy on their hands and knees. The boys paused when they saw Susan and Midge. Then they dropped down on all fours beside them. One was fair and one was dark and the fair one said, "You 'ave found somezing, yes?"

The dark one gave him a friendly shove which nearly sent him out of the train on to the platform. "Hansli not spik English good," the dark one said. "He mean, you 'ave lost nozzing, no?"

"No," said Midge, "we're just crouching here for the fun of it."

The boys looked puzzled.

"Oh do shut up, Midge," said Susan. "You'll give the whole game away——!"

"A game?" said the boys and looked relieved. The

English, they knew, were always playing games. That explained everything. "A game!"

"No!" said Susan. "No, I should think not! It's no game! No, this is serious!"

The boys immediately got the idea that the English girls had lost something called a *serious*: they hadn't the vaguest idea what they were looking for but they obligingly began sniffing round like a couple of terriers. It was rather crowded in the confined space between the seats and everybody kept bumping or kicking or poking an elbow into everybody else. The confusion wasn't helped by Susan who in her kindly way decided that this was a good opportunity for improving the boys' English. She kept picking up pieces of their anatomy or their clothing and enunciating the English name for it very loudly and clearly.

Then what seemed to be the main body of schoolboys surged into the carriage. Those in front just saved themselves from trampling on the four on the floor. Hansli said something in Swiss and all the boys grinned and got down on their hands and knees.

Midge struggled up through the mass of arms and legs and bodies. "Seems to me there are enough people looking for something that doesn't exist," she muttered, and sat down. So she was in a good position for seeing the next person to arrive on the scene, none other than the hot-tempered little schoolmaster who had boxed Susan's ears.

He began shouting something and twelve heads shot up and a clamour of explanation broke out. He was just lifting his hand to distribute a few well-earned cuffs when he caught sight of Susan, red in the face, hair dishevelled, looking up from her crouching position on the floor between the seats. He blushed red and thrust his itching hand in his pocket. He bowed coldly. "Fräulein!" he said.

Susan, feeling a perfect ass, ducked her head in reply.

"You have lost something, Fräulein?"

Susan cast an anguished glance at Midge. She couldn't just tell a barefaced lie, but she couldn't, *couldn't* tell this cross little man that they hadn't lost anything but were grovelling about on the floor in this shameful way in order to hide from the ticket-collector.

Midge came to the rescue, thinking that the less heard from Susan the better. "Well," she said very rapidly, hoping that the little schoolmaster wouldn't quite follow what she was saying, "to be honest, we haven't exactly lost anything but we haven't any TICKETS."

"Tickets!" exclaimed the little man. "Ah! You have lost your tickets——!"

"Well you said it, not me," said Midge under her breath.

The little man snapped his fingers. "Come boys! Hansli, Anton, search! Search! Search till you find!"

"That'll test them," muttered Midge.

The carriage was filling up by this time. The boys, who seemed to have the same sort of traits as English small boys, made as much commotion as possible, crawling round people's legs, pushing each other, looking in the most impossible places, shouting, laughing—the confusion was terrible.

However, when the train moved off and no tickets had been found, the schoolmaster made his flock sit down. "When we are arriving at the bottom, Fräulein," he said, "we are searching again. I arrange——"

Susan grinned feebly and said thank you very much in a small voice. Midge settled herself in her usual corner and closed her eyes. After a little this inertia began to get on Susan's nerves. "Och Midge," she said, "*do* wake up! We've got to think of a plan!"

"*He* said he was going to arrange it," said Midge. "Let's see what he arranges before we start on plans."

"Well at least," said Susan, "you ought to take advantage of all those free rides. Enjoy the scenery! Look at the lake! And the flowers! And, and, and the cows——!"

"I'm not so interested in the cows after seeing them for the fifth time," said Midge.

At Vitznau the boys were all eagerness to start the search again for these famous tickets, but the little schoolmaster began to get agitated about missing the boat. He hummed and hawed for a bit then he said to Susan, "Fräulein, I am having two tickets of boys who are not. Please do me the honour of accepting this tickets——"

Midge thought, I'm going off my nut—first of all non-existent tickets and now non-existent boys. Susan cried, "Oh, *thank* you! But you see, we need tickets for the boat too and we haven't any money and

Uncle Charles has our return tickets and he's some-where on the mountain, walking down——"

"This tickets are taking you to Lucerne," said the schoolmaster and waved away their thanks.

"Well," said Midge as they proudly showed their tickets to the ticket collector and walked down to the pier, "that slap on the ear was worth it, don't you think?"

"Oh gosh, *yes*," said Susan. "I must say, I never thought I'd live to see the day when I'd be grateful to *that* little man!"

CHAPTER THREE

FRÄULEIN AMACHER'S POUND OF TEA

OF COURSE the walking party were disgustingly
pleased with themselves and raved about the beauties
of the mountain path, the pretty chalets they had
passed, the alpine flowers they had seen, the stupendous
views of the lake, the little wayside shrines; but Susan
and Midge had their revenge next morning when the
others were all stiff and sore from the use of unaccus-
tomed muscles and Aunt Lucy couldn't walk downstairs without uttering loud groans on every step.

"Thank goodness we've planned a quiet day," she
said. "Exploring Rosendorf first and then our visit
to Lucerne——"

"Susie and I thought we'd swim this morning," said
Midge.

"Swim!" said Charlotte. "I'd think I'd break in
two."

However they all managed a swim without any
such disastrous effects; and about eleven they set off
for Lucerne—a little late for the boat as usual, and
Aunt Lucy saying that the boat would just have to go
without her for she could *not* hurry when every step
was agony.

Lucerne was lovely, built at one end of the lake
with the river Reuss running through it, with a
crown of little towers and full of nice old twisty
streets and ancient squares with flower-decked foun-

tains and houses with pictures painted on them and two old covered wooden bridges, one with scenes from the town's history painted inside on the arches, the other with very gloomy scenes of Death—and of course with lots and lots of shops with an even greater variety of carvings, embroideries, musical boxes, cuckoo-clocks and gorgeous postcards. They found the most delightful little café for lunch. It overlooked a quiet backwater of the river, near one of the old bridges and the town mill; boxes of flowers edged the low parapet, swans and ducks came up for scraps, a nearby fountain splashed gently. The menu was very conveniently translated into English; because she liked the sound of it Susan had 2 *Weggli und* 1 *Gipfel* which was rendered as 2 *Buns and* 1 *Roll* and everybody had a great deal of cream.

Fräulein Amacher's flat was in a strange old house overlooking the river. On one wall was painted an enormous family tree with little portraits of members of the family and pictures illustrating their deeds. Susan was fascinated and would have gazed at it for hours, but Midge said that she wouldn't like *her* family plastered up on a wall for tourists to gape at, and Uncle Charles said that unfortunately their family wasn't grand enough to be up on a wall and Aunt Lucy said would they all please come *now* or they would be late for tea at Fräulein Amacher's.

Fräulein Amacher's flat was two stairs up; two little green doors stood side by side, one with a shining brass plate that said *G. Amacher.* "I wonder what the *G* stands for," said Susan idly as they waited for the door to be opened.

Fräulein Amacher was a tall handsome elderly lady with grey hair. She flung wide the door and cried, "Ah! How delighted I am to see you! And have you brought my pound of tea?"

"Oh yes," said Aunt Lucy. "Where is the tea, girls?"

Susan and Midge and Charlotte looked at each other. "Susan's got it," said Midge.

"No I haven't!" said Susan. "I put it on your bed. I thought you'd taken it."

"I didn't take it," said Midge, "I thought you had——"

Aunt Lucy looked vexed. She apologised profusely to Fräulein Amacher who said that it didn't matter a bit, any time would do, and Susan said that she would bring it to Fräulein Amacher the very next day. Fräulein Amacher laughed and said there was no hurry and ushered them all into the flat. Susan and Bill came last, and as Susan was stepping in she happened to glance at the other door. It was closing, very, very gently. It gave Susan quite a turn, as if someone had been standing behind it, listening. She turned to Bill, to tell him, hoping he would say that she was talking a lot of nonsense, but Bill had gone in. With a last puzzled look at the other door, Susan went inside too.

Fräulein Amacher was most interesting and told them a lot about Switzerland and Lucerne and her flat in this old building which had been the town house of a noble family in bygone days, and about Rosendorf and the Chalet du Lac where they were staying. The Stockers, who owned it, were a young couple and they had only just started their hotel. Fräulein Amacher had been a schoolmistress and Frau Stocker had been one of her pupils so she was anxious that they should do well. "That is why I write the letters for them," she said. "I give them lessons in English in winter but in summer of course there is not time—they both speak quite well but they do not yet write English well so I write for them. They would like many more English visitors——"

"But the hotel is full!" said Aunt Lucy.

"Yes it is full now, in July and August, but they would like it full also in June and September. No, it must become known to English visitors and then it will always be full."

"We'll tell all our friends!" said Susan, wondering what else she could do to help the Stockers.

They had tea in a room filled with heavy dark old Swiss furniture overlooking the rushing milky-jade waters of the Reuss. It was a sumptuous tea, bread and butter and cherry jam followed by a selection of all the most luscious Swiss cakes such as they had drooled over in the pastry-cooks' windows, finishing up with what seemed about twenty different varieties of chocolate bars. Bill wrote their names down in his notebook for future reference and Fräulein Amacher beamed at their enjoyment. "I know that English people always like the five o'clock tea," she said.

As they, bloated with food, were rising to go, Fräulein Amacher, who had been telling them of all the excursions round about Lake Lucerne that they must not miss, said with some slight hesitation, "I wonder if I might ask of you a very great favour?"

"Of course," said Aunt Lucy recklessly, "anything!"

"Well," said Fräulein Amacher, "I hope that it will not be a great inconvenience to you, but I wonder if you would allow a small boy to travel back with you to London?"

"But of *course*——" said Aunt Lucy.

"He has been here on holiday and I could put him in charge of the air hostess, but I should feel happier if I knew that he was with someone I know——"

Aunt Lucy and Uncle Charles said that nothing could be easier, they were only too glad to do anything to help Fräulein Amacher and only wished that she had asked them to do something really difficult! Susan, who happened to be looking at Fräulein Amacher, noticed a peculiar expression flit across her face. It was gone in an instant, Fräulein Amacher was smiling. "Let us hope that this will not prove difficult," she said.

Fräulein Amacher made arrangements with Dr. Carmichael about booking a seat on the same plane for the boy, then they all said good-bye and Susan and the Carmichaels went away. They crossed the Reuss by the footbridge between the old *Rathaus*, which Aunt Lucy said meant town hall, and Fräulein Amacher's mediaeval palace. Half-way across they stopped to look back and wave to Fräulein Amacher who was leaning out of her window waving briskly. At the next window stood a motionless figure, watching. As the girls waved, the figure drew back and a hand closed the shutters. The same shivery feeling came over Susan that she had felt as she stood at Fräulein Amacher's door and watched that other door stealthily closing. "We're being watched!" she thought.

"Honestly," said Susan, "I don't care what any of you say or how much you jeer, I think there's something sinister about Fräulein Amacher! And as we're mixed up in it somehow, I think it's our business to find out what it is——"

It was the following morning and Bill and the girls had taken out one of the hotel rowing-boats and were having a gentle row on the lake, with Susan and Bill at the oars. When Susan had finished delivering her few remarks in a defiant voice, Charlotte said, "Now look here, Susie, it's all very well at home having you interfering and poking your nose into other people's business, but you'd better not try anything like that here. Before you know where you are you'll be starting an international incident——"

"What's an international incident?" asked Bill.

"Well," said Charlotte impatiently, "any kind of bother between countries that gets a bit out of hand and the high-ups in the government have to sort it out——"

"Frankly, I don't believe that Susie's important enough to be an international incident," Midge said in her tiredest voice.

"If you ask me," said Bill, "Susie could easily be an international incident. Susie's always getting out of hand."

"Och away, Bill," said Susan, giving him a friendly shove with her foot in the small of his back which nearly capsized the boat, "I haven't done a thing!"

"No, but you're talking very wildly," said Charlotte severely. "Saying things about people. You'll land yourself in court for slander before you're finished."

Susan thought that her future, causing international incidents and landing in a court of law for saying things about people, sounded quite varied and interesting but at the same time very unlikely. "All I said," she said defensively, "was that Fräulein Amacher was a sinister character."

"Sinister in what way?" said Bill.

"I think she's a secret agent," said Susan.

Her cousins made rude and derisive noises. Old Susie had had some pretty wild notions in her day, but this struck them as one of the wildest. Midge shook her head. "No, no, Susie," she said, "you're making it all up this time——"

"I am not then," Susan said indignantly. "I didn't make up the pound of tea, did I, and all that spying that was going on from the person next door that I told you about——?"

"Well," said Midge, gamely trying to follow Susan's so-called reasoning, "that doesn't make Fräulein Amacher a spy. If anyone's a spy, it's the person next door——"

"No," said Susan. "the person next door is the counter-spy——"

The others started laughing again and Susan grinned good-naturedly. "Oh you can laugh," she said, "but I've got a feeling in my bones that there's something queer going on and you know as well as I do that when I get that feeling in my bones that there's something queer going on, then there *is* something queer going on——"

The others looked unconvinced. Susan, they were bound to admit, *had* in the past managed to straighten out some tangles in people's lives, but that was more by good luck that good guidance. And she had certainly never had such a dotty idea as this. Midge thought that it was time the voice of reason spoke up. "You can't just sit there and say that Fräulein Amacher is a secret agent," she said. "Where's your evidence?"

"The tea," said Susan calmly. "You can't tell me that anybody would ask total strangers to take the trouble to bring tea from England just for the sake of the tea. You can get tea here—you saw that notice in the Confiserie Hofmann, 5 O'CLOCK TEA—up on the wall in great big letters. And you heard Fräulein Amacher yourself, the very first words she spoke to us were did you bring my pound of tea. I've been thinking it out and I reckon there's a secret document hidden in the tea. Or something."

"Susan," said Charlotte, "how silly can you get? Just because you don't like tea yourself doesn't mean that other people don't think that it's worth a bit of trouble. Aunt Lucy says that tea on the Continent is usually frightful. I think it's quite probable that someone like Fräulein Amacher who has lived in England would just long for some decent English tea."

"Nonsense," said Susan in a very pig-headed way. "It's quite obvious to me that the tea is being used as a cover. All that correspondence that she does for the hotel too. That could all be a blind. She could be getting every English visitor who comes over to bring a pound of tea with a secret document hidden in every packet. Or," she went on, anxious to be fair, "she might not be a secret agent, she might be an ordinary straightforward smuggler. The tea could be stuffed with diamonds or stolen jewels or dangerous drugs or——"

But Susan had overdone it this time. Even Bill, usually her most faithful ally, was laughing. "Until I see Fräulein Amacher in a false beard," he said, "I refuse to believe that she's a secret agent—or a smuggler!"

"So stop blethering, Susie dear," said Charlotte.

"Stop blethering and pay attention to what you're doing," said Midge who was in the bow, idly dabbling her fingers in the water and trying to entice a couple of swans to come closer. "There's a steamer coming down the lake from Vitznau and if you ask me it's getting rather close. Don't you think——?"

Susan glanced back over her shoulder. When she saw the steamer looming horribly close she gave a yelp of panic and began to row frenziedly. But she overdid it, caught a crab, lost her oar and fell over backwards on to Midge's feet. This was very upsetting for Bill who, however, managed to keep his head and began to fish for Susan's oar, nnfortunately hitting Susan a smart crack on the head as she struggled up from the bottom of the boat. Susan yelped again, Charlotte shouted at both of them impatiently and Midge muttered, "Does the idea of being cut in two by this enormous great boat not worry any of you?" It worried them a great deal—Bill fished feverishly for the oar and eventually rescued it, Susan grabbed it and she and Bill began to row hurriedly and raggedly for the shore. The steamer altered course, hooted furiously and swept on towards Rosendorf pier.

As the little boat tossed agitatedly in the steamer's wash, Bill and the girls sighed gustily with relief.

"Phew!" exclaimed Susan, shipping her oar and fanning herself vigorously, "I thought that my last moment had come!"

"You can say *that* again," Bill agreed.

"Then for heaven's sake let us get nearer the shore," said Charlotte, "I'll feel safer there!"

"You and Midge row then for a change," Bill suggested.

"Me row?" said Midge. "I couldn't. I'm trembling like a leaf."

"Actually I don't mind rowing," said Susan, "I prefer it really—except when a ghastly great steamer comes bearing down on us——"

They were by this time opposite the pretty brown chalet in the wonderful gardens that they had noticed the previous day. There were mattresses and *duvets* hanging out of the windows, airing. From where they were, low down on the water, the gardens were partly screened by low walls, which annoyed Susan, who liked to see everything that was going on. "We got a better view from the steamer," she remarked.

"I think that anyone who mentions the word *steamer* for at least a week should be fined a franc," said Charlotte. "Let's get as near to the shore as we can without actually running aground, and row quietly back to the Chalet for a swim."

CHAPTER FOUR

DANGER IN THE KAPELLGASSE

THAT MORNING some friends of Aunt Lucy and Dr. Carmichael called Chester, who were on holiday at Lucerne, were coming to spend the day with them at Rosendorf.

They very kindly brought a luscious box of chocolates with them for the young people who thought that the least they could do in return for such kindness was to disappear after lunch and leave the grown-ups to their boring talk.

"What shall we do?" asked Charlotte.

"Lie down somewhere in the shade and eat chocolates," suggested Midge.

"Och away, Midge," said Susan. "You get lazier all the time. One of these days you'll get too lazy to breathe. Let's take Fräulein Amacher's pound of tea to her."

"Good idea," said Bill. "And we can go and see the Lion of Lucerne at the same time."

"The Lion of Lucerne?" asked Susan. "A real lion?"

"It's a monument," said Bill. "Put up to commemorate the Swiss Guard in Paris in the time of the French Revolution who all died guarding Louis the Sixteenth in the Tuileries Palace from the revolutionary mob. Louis quite forgot to mention to the guard that he was slipping out the back way and they didn't need to die at all——"

"Is that true?" asked Susan.

"Well, it's in my book," said Bill.

"Jings," exploded Susan, "what a thing to do! He jolly well deserved to get his head chopped off and I'm very glad he did. I wish I'd been there to see him——"

"I can just picture Susan," said Charlotte, "sitting at the foot of the guillotine, with her knitting, counting the heads, like the old women in *A Tale of Two Cities*."

"Never," said Midge, "she'd be right up there on the guillotine telling the chap who worked it how he ought to do it and interfering with the mechanism——"

"Och away," said Susan, grinning.

Aunt Lucy thought that the trip to Lucerne was quite a good idea, just as long as they took care of themselves, didn't spend too much on ices and chocolate and didn't miss the last boat back to Rosendorf. The girls and Bill promised that they would pay attention to all these matters, collected the parcel of tea and set off.

Having arrived at Lucerne they passed three very enticing cafés on the way to Fräulein Amacher's flat, but nobly determined to resist temptation—at least until after delivering the parcel. They stood at Fräulein Amacher's neat little door and rang the bell. And as they rang, it seemed to Susan, who was watching it, that the door of the next flat opened the tiniest crack. There was no answer to their ring. They rang again. There was no answer.

"Oh bother," said Midge, "she's not in. Dragging up all those stairs for nothing."

This was something they hadn't expected. They stood wondering what to do; and Susan stood and looked at the crack in the other door. Suddenly she jumped and clutched Midge's arm. She could see something in the tiny opening—and that something was an eye.

The others were still arguing about the pound of tea and what to do with it. Susan began to pull Midge's arm, saying, "Let's go home. Now. This minute. Let's go——" when the eye disappeared and the door of the flat adjoining Fräulein Amacher's suddenly opened and a young woman appeared. She was tall and quite pretty, Susan admitted to herself, in a hard glittering sort of way, but Susan didn't like her at all. She couldn't forget that eye.

The sight of the deputation on the doorstep seemed to surprise the young woman although Susan didn't see why it should for she had been watching them for ages. She spoke in Swiss and when they all looked blank she said in English, "You are searching for Fräulein Amacher perhaps?"

"Yes," they said.

"Oh, I am so sor-r-ry. But she has gone away."

"Gone away?" they said blankly.

"Yes, she has gone away for a few days."

"Oh," said Charlotte, "then perhaps you could give us her address?"

"I am sor-r-ry," the young lady said again, rolling her r's, "she has not given me her address."

"What a pity," Charlotte said, "I wish I knew where

Fräulein Amacher had gone because we have a parcel for her——"

The young woman smiled. "I shall be only too honoured to keep the parcel for you and give it to Fräulein Amacher when she come back," she said.

"Will you? Oh good," said Midge and held out the pound of tea. This seemed an excellent solution to their problem, so that everybody was extremely surprised when Susan very rudely snatched the parcel out of Midge's hands.

"Oh no," she said, "please don't bother! It's quite all right, we'll bring it another day——"

The Carmichaels all looked very embarrassed, the young woman's bright smile stiffened a little but she only said pleasantly, "As you wish——"

"Well—er—then good-bye, Frau—Fräulein——" said Charlotte in an embarrassed mutter.

"I am Frau Tannenbaum," the young woman said, smiling again. "It has give me great pleasure to meet you and I hope that we will meet again soon."

The Carmichaels did not know what to say to this, so they mumbled as politely as they could and went away.

They began scolding Susan before they reached the bottom of the stairs, and were still at it when they left the old house.

"Honestly, Susie, *so* rude," said Charlotte. They began to cross the Kornmarkt.

"I don't know why you had to interfere," said Midge. "Now we'll have to come again another day. Lucerne is heaven, but honestly we don't want to spend our whole holiday coming to Lucerne with Fräulein

Amacher's pound of tea. Why on earth wouldn't you let me give it to Frau Whatever-her-name-is?"

"Because she's a counter-spy!" said Bill in a sarcastic voice.

"Exactly!" said Susan, and everybody laughed rudely. "Oh you can laugh," said Susan. "But she was watching us, you know, long before she opened the door!"

"*Watching* us?"

"Yes, the door was open a wee bit; she had her eye to the crack and I saw her eye glitter!"

The Carmichaels roared again at that, and Charlotte recited a bit out of *The Ancient Mariner* about a *long grey beard and glittering eye*, but Susan only said imperturbably that Frau What's-her-name hadn't a long grey beard but that she definitely had a glittering eye with which she had watched them. And she led the way to the Kapellgasse.

This was an ancient, very narrow, very busy little street which led from the Kornmarkt to the Schwanenplatz, and at the busiest, narrowest bit was one of the three cafés which had caught the eye of Midge. It didn't look much, just a small unpretentious entrance, but the cakes in the window were, Charlotte said, out of this world. Susan and the Carmichaels stood on the pavement on the opposite side of the road and looked across at it. "Well, come on then, let's go there," said Bill. "Too much talk and not enough action about you girls."

There was plenty of action about Susan two seconds later, for as she stood on the edge of the pavement waiting for a car to pass she suddenly felt a strong push in the small of her back and she would have been under the wheels of the oncoming car if someone standing near hadn't grabbed her arm and dragged her back to safety. So enthusiastically did this person hang on to her that he almost wrenched Fräulein Amacher's precious pound of tea out of her grasp. But Susan wrenched just as strongly and clasped the tea grimly to her chest and stared at her rescuer, white-faced.

"Oh heavens, *Susie*, oh Monsieur, Herr—thank you—*merci—danke*——" Charlotte babbled to the young man who had pulled Susan back on to the pavement. "Heavens, Susan, you might have been killed!"

The young man, who had flaxen hair so fair that it was nearly white, did not wait to be thanked. "It is nothing," he said, and was gone. With Charlotte holding Susan firmly by one arm and Midge holding her by the other and Bill guarding from behind, they safely negotiated the street and went into the café. They went up some narrow steep stairs and found a table in a quiet corner of the tiny place. Susan, weak at the knees, fell into a seat, her face still chalk-white.

They ordered *café glacé*, a heavenly delicacy, a cross between iced coffee and coffee ice, very expensive but justified, they felt, in the circumstances; and as Susan spooned the delicious stuff and savoured its creaminess on her tongue, her face recovered its normal rosy hue and the spirits of the others rose accordingly.

"Whew!" exclaimed Midge. "I thought your last hour had come, Susie. I just pictured us picking the bits off the wheels of that car——"

"I don't expect you would have been actually killed," said Bill encouragingly, "the car wasn't going fast enough——"

Susan glanced up from her *café glacé*. "Just maimed for life, I suppose," she said rather sourly.

"Of course not," said Charlotte soothingly. "But," she couldn't resist adding in a very elder-sisterly way, "you should take more care—tripping over your big feet like that in that narrow little street you could easily have been under the car——"

Susan put down her spoon and glared at Charlotte. "I like that!" she said. "I didn't trip! I was pushed!"

The others all instantly and indignantly denied having laid a finger on Susan, intentionally or otherwise. "I don't think you should talk like that," said Charlotte severely. "It's very ungrateful. None of us pushed you and there was no one else near except that man who saved your life——"

"Saved my life!" said Susan. "It was he who pushed me!"

The Carmichaels goggled at her. "The shock has turned her brain," Midge said at last sadly. "You've got it muddled, Susie, he didn't *push* you, he grabbed you!"

"He pushed me first and then he grabbed me," said Susan. "At least, it was Fräulein Amacher's pound of tea that he really grabbed but I was holding on to it too tightly for him——"

They all burst out: "Oh, *honestly*, Susan!"

"What on *earth* would he want with Fräulein Amacher's pound of tea!"

"No, no, Susie, that's carrying a love of tea *too* far——"

"You're so taken up with all this rubbish about poor old Fräulein Amacher that you've invented——"

"I *told* you that the shock had turned her brain!"

"If you mean the stuff that rattles about between her ears, I don't know if you could actually call it *brain*——"

"You're all very funny and I'm killing myself laughing," said Susan, "but I wish you'd all be quiet. I'm thinking——"

This rather peevish tone from their usually sweet-tempered Susan was so unexpected that it silenced the Carmichaels immediately. They went on quietly eating their *café glacé*. They must make allowances for old Susie, they realised, for she had had a very nasty shock.

Susan finished her ice in silence, sighed blissfully, licked her lips and announced, "Well, I've thought, and I've decided. We must open the parcel. I know it's not ours, but it is in our possession and I think that we're quite justified in finding out what's inside it when so many people are so anxious to lay their hands on it—Fräulein Amacher and Frau What's-her-name and this murderous man——"

"Now listen, Susan——" Charlotte began but Susan wouldn't let her go on.

"Just listen to *me*," she said. "I know as surely as I'm sitting here that I was pushed off that pavement. It was all deliberate. He pushed me off so that I'd get a fright and then when I'd got a fright and was off my guard he pretended to save me and grabbed the parcel at the same time. Nearly got it too, but something made me clutch on to it. If it had been you he was pushing around you would have jolly soon known whether he was trying to save you or grab the parcel—And Bill," she went on, seeing Bill open his mouth and taking breath to speak, "it's no use asking me how he knew we had the parcel because I don't know. Probably he has been following us around for days——"

Charlotte gave an exasperated sigh, but she evidently knew when she was beaten because she said, "Open it if you like. Only not here—I can't picture us sitting here smothered in tea-leaves like the babes in the wood——"

Bill consulted Charlotte's watch and then one of his innumerable pamphlets. "Shall we go back to Rosendorf, then?" he said. "Only thing is, we've just missed the four o'clock boat——"

Charlotte did murmur something about the Lion of Lucerne which, after all, they had come to see, but nobody paid any attention. Midge and Bill, although they wouldn't admit that they were convinced by Susan's reasoning (if you could call it reasoning, said Bill) seemed to be just as anxious to see inside Fräulein Amacher's parcel as Susan. "We could go along that promenade by the side of the lake where the big hotels and grand shops are and find a quiet seat," Bill suggested.

"Not *too* far along," Midge muttered.

They sat down on the first empty bench they came to, under the shade of some trees and looking over the smooth and sparkling waters of the lake, where the swans sailed lazily and tiny boats skimmed like white butterflies, to the wild mountain slopes and the snow-tipped peaks beyond. Not that either Susan or the Carmichaels had any eyes for the scenery; they were gazing intently at Fräulein Amacher's parcel while Susan fumbled with the knots. "They're jolly stiff, these knots," said Susan and bent down and pulled at them with sharp teeth.

When the paper came off, there lay a pound packet of tea. At least the packet said tea, Earl Grey's Mixture, exactly like the packets they had seen often in Aunt Lucy's cupboard, the tea which she kept for best. It also felt like tea they all agreed as they prodded it.

"Well, there you are," said Charlotte. "Tea."

But Susan wasn't beaten yet. "There must be something inside," she said and picked carefully with her finger-nail at the Scotch tape that sealed the packet.

"Still tea," said Charlotte, when the packet was opened.

Susan pushed exploring fingers into the tea. She gave a little excited gasp and drew out two things. One was a sealed and addressed envelope, the other was a British passport.

They stared down at the familiar, dignified blue and gold. The space at the bottom said 1646590 and the space at the top said *Rudi Panacek*. Susan opened it and they stared at the photograph of a young boy, solemn, thin-faced, big-eyed. Nobody spoke—until at last Susan said, "This is a passport!"

"Yes we can see that," murmured Midge.

"Gosh!" said Susan. "This is worse than I thought!

It's absolutely deadly serious to traffic in forged passports!"

"What makes you think it's forged?" asked Midge.

"Well, look at it," said Susan, turning the stiff pages. "All the pages that say *visas*, are blank! It has never been used! If it were an ordinary passport it would have something stamped on it! People only get a passport if they're going abroad and the minute they get abroad their passports are stamped! This one hasn't been stamped at all! I bet it's forged!"

"What would anyone want with a forged passport?" Bill asked.

"Well," said Susan, "the same as anyone would want with a real passport. To go abroad."

Midge said in a bored voice, "Why not just *get* a real passport, then? Surely it would be easier than all this larking about with pounds of tea?"

"But if you couldn't! If you were in some country where they wouldn't let you go abroad and you wanted to go abroad!"

"Yes, but Switzerland isn't like that," said Midge, reasonably enough.

"No, that's true," said Susan, slightly dashed. "But other countries in Europe are," she went on, cheering up again. "All those places behind the Iron Curtain—lots of people want to get out of those countries!" She paused for a second and added, "Jings! D'you know what *I* think?"

The Carmichaels all said no in hopeless sort of voices.

"I think that Fräulein Amacher must be a member of some kind of underground movement, and she's

S.I.   C not smuggling goods, she's smuggling people! Smuggling souls!" she said, quite carried away by this high-sounding phrase.

Charlotte said coldly, "Susan you're gifted with a very fertile imagination and you're now warming up nicely, but you can just cool down again. I never heard such a lot of rot in my life."

Susan looked hurt, like a bouncing puppy whose friendly overtures don't get the welcome it expects. "Don't you think I'm right?" she asked in a disappointed voice.

"Frankly," said Charlotte, "no."

"Smuggling souls!" said Midge and gave a little snort of laughter.

Bill said slowly, "I know it sounds completely dotty, but actually, why should this passport come to Fräulein Amacher in this secret way unless there's something queer about it? It seems to me she must want it to get somebody into England——"

"Yes but this is a small boy's passport!" Midge objected.

"Oh, a forger can soon alter that!" said Susan airily.

Charlotte said, "The whole thing not only *sounds* dotty, it *is* dotty——"

"Don't forget that *some* of Susie's dotty ideas have turned out to be quite right," said Bill.

"Yes, but not this one," said Charlotte. "*Hon*estly!"

"Well, what *does* it all mean then?" said Susan.

None of the Carmichaels had the faintest idea what it all meant and said so. Then Bill asked, "Where's the other thing that was in the tea?" Susan held out the envelope. On it was written *Frau Weber, Wissifluh, Vierwaldstättersee.*

"What does *that* mean?" said Midge.

Bill said, "Vierwaldstättersee is the German name for the Lake of Lucerne, it means the Lake of the Four Cantons, and I *think* Wissifluh is the name of a place——" He pulled his map of the lake out of his pocket and studied it. "Yes! I was right, there it is, above Vitznau. There's a cable-railway up to it. That must be the place whose lights we see from Rosendorf, at night, half-way up the mountain——"

Susan opened her mouth to speak and Charlotte quickly said, "*No*, Susan, we could *not* go up there poking around, interfering in people's business!"

"I never said a word!" said Susan.

"No, but that's what you were planning," said Charlotte. "Put the passport and the letter back in the tea and wrap it up for goodness' sake and keep it until we see Fräulein Amacher and can give it to her her——"

"Yes, but that's just it!" cried Susan.

"What's just it?"

"When are we going to see Fräulein Amacher?"

"Well *I* don't know," said Charlotte impatiently. "In a day or two, I suppose, when she comes back——"

"*If* she comes back, you mean!" said Susan in a deep and dramatic voice.

"*Hon*estly, Susan, *now* what bee have you got in your bonnet?"

"No bee," said Susan in rather an offended voice. "It's common sense. You don't really think that

Fräulein Amacher has just gone calmly off for a couple of days' holiday, do you? Without a word? Without a message? No, no, her enemies have caught up with her and she has been kidnapped. That woman next door, Frau Tannenbaum or whatever her name is, is one of the gang and the white-haired man is another. She was left to get the parcel and when we wouldn't hand it over she sent her accomplice to push me under a car——"

This time the Carmichaels didn't even argue, they just laughed. Susan laughed too, eventually, and said good-naturedly, "Okay, laugh, but I still think that something has happened to poor old Fräulein Amacher, and I think that we ought to *try* to find her at least. I don't see why we shouldn't go up to Wissifluh or whatever it's called. It would be jolly nice to go up to a little mountain village in a cable-railway—we could take a picnic—we needn't interfere in anybody's business, we could just nose around a little——"

"Oh help!" said Midge.

"Don't forget," Bill said again, "that Susan is *sometimes* right——"

Midge said, "Bill, you sound like a boring old gipsy's warning, *Susan's sometimes right*——"

"Well she is," said Bill. "Not very often, I admit, but——"

"Och away, you cheeky thing," said Susan. She put the envelope, which was nice and fat and which she was longing to open only she was quite certain that Charlotte wouldn't allow *that*, and the passport back in among the tea and wrapped the parcel up again. They all got up and made their way slowly along the promenade and across the bridge to the quays. By the time they were on the boat she had persuaded Charlotte that it wouldn't do any harm just to go up to Wissifluh for a *picnic*.

CHAPTER FIVE

LOOKING FOR FRÄULEIN AMACHER

THEY HAD a delightful swim in the cool waters of the lake when they returned to the Chalet du Lac. And after that Susan dressed with great speed for dinner, and while Midge was still milling round putting on a clean frock and brushing her hair, Susan sought out Frau Stocker and asked her if she had had a message from Fräulein Amacher. Frau Stocker had had no message and said that she was very surprised indeed to hear that Fräulein Amacher had gone away for a few days without telling her—there was the hotel correspondence for one thing, and there was a letter there from some English people waiting for a reply— Gosh! thought Susan. This is my chance! She took a deep breath and asked Frau Stocker if she wouldn't allow her to reply. "It would be an awful pity if you lost some customers or visitors or whatever you call them," she said. "You could tell me exactly what you want to say, about dates and so on, and I'll write the letter. Midge can help me—she's a frightfully good speller——"

Frau Stocker laughed and said that it was very kind of Susan to trouble herself with the hotel's affairs and Susan said earnestly that it was no trouble, that she would *like* to do it, and Frau Stocker said all right, it was agreed then, if Susan would come to the office with her she would give her the letter and tell her what to say.

When Susan told the others at dinner-time Midge thought that she was mad. "You mean to say you're going to *write* a *letter*? Write a letter that you don't have to write?" she said.

"Everybody doesn't look on letter-writing as a kind of slow torture like you do, Midge," Aunt Lucy said. "I think it's very kind of Susan to take an interest in the hotel——"

The others giggled and Midge said that seemed a jolly queer way to describe Susan's nosy, interfering ways, but Susan looked smug. She said, "Aunt Lucy we were thinking that it would be quite fun to have a picnic to-morrow at Wissifluh——"

"Vissyflew?" asked Aunt Lucy.

"W-i-s-s-i-f-l-u-h," Susan spelt it out. "It's that little place that we can see above Vitznau. It looks jolly nice all lighted up——"

"Well we're not going to see it all lighted up if we go for a picnic," Midge muttered.

Aunt Lucy looked rather guilty. "Well as a matter of fact, the Chesters have asked us to go to their hotel for lunch to-morrow——"

"Oh crumbs, Aunt Lucy," said Bill, "not Lucerne again! I mean, Lucerne is jolly nice but all that these girls do is rush from shop to shop—I wouldn't know why because as far as I can see all the shops have the same sort of things——"

"Well, I'm sorry," said Aunt Lucy, "but to-morrow is the Chesters' last day——"

"But Bill and the girls needn't come with us," said

Uncle Charles; so it was arranged to everyone's satisfaction that Aunt Lucy and Uncle Charles should go to Lucerne and the others should go to Wissifluh.

When they reached Vitznau next morning with the usual crowd of people who were going up the Rigi they couldn't at first find the station of the cable-railway that would take them up the mountain. They could see the cable, a silver thread as thin as a spider's web shining in the sun.

"I thought that all we should have to do would be to follow the crowds," said Midge. "But there don't seem to be any crowds, except for the Rigi."

"If we keep the cable in sight we ought to be able to find the end of it," Charlotte suggested.

"Why not just ask someone?" said Bill.

"Because we don't know the language," said Midge.

"Gosh, you don't need to know the language to say *Wissifluh*," said Bill.

Susan said nothing. She was, as a matter of fact, beginning to feel rather nervous of this cable-car to Wissifluh. She had discovered on the expedition up the Rigi that she didn't like heights very much, and that silver thread against the blue sky looked horribly high, *horribly* frail. And yet, how to get up to that eagle's eyrie which was Wissifluh and which they could see clinging to the face of the mountain, unless by cable-car? She wondered whether she could call the whole thing off? But then, she *wanted* to get up to Wissifluh to see if there was a clue to Fräulein Amacher's sudden disappearance—besides Midge and Charlotte would think she had gone off her rocker—all the Carmichaels seemed to have splendid heads for heights, she thought. Oh, well, perhaps, the cable-car wouldn't be so bad——

Bill meantime had stopped a passer-by and was now leading the way confidently through the village, past the neat chalets in their gardens. "That's the station, I should think," said Bill, pointing to a large shed.

"Funny looking station," said Charlotte looking round. A large wheel whirled round above their heads from which came a cable making queer clanking noises.

"No train," said Midge.

Susan still said nothing. She was liking the idea of this cable-car less and less.

Bill's inspection of the station didn't take long as there was nothing to inspect. "Hey," he said, "here's a telephone. What d'you reckon that's for?"

Midge suggested that it was for summoning the ambulance when the cable-car crashed down the hillside to the bottom, which didn't improve Susan's peace of mind. Charlotte told Midge absently not to be silly and they all crowded round a very antiquated telephone which hung on the wall. Beside it was a notice in three languages. They supposed one of them to be English as it gave helpful suggestions like *Ring onc. Pic up receivre.* Eventually Charlotte said doubtfully, "I think the idea is that when you want the cable-car you have to telephone up to the top for it."

"For goodness' sake!" said Midge. "Go on then Susie, ring for the thing."

"Who, me?" Susan squeaked.

"You're the one who wanted to go to Wissifluh."

"I didn't par*ti*cularly want to go to Wissifluh," said Susan in an offhand voice. "In fact I don't care if we give up the whole idea and go home——"

Midge looked at her in surprise; but meantime Bill had tackled the telephone. He picked up the receiver and wound a handle. "Oh hallo," they heard him saying, "I mean *Bonjour*, I mean *Grüezi*" (this was the universal greeting in Switzerland, the one word that they had all learnt) " *Voulez-vous*—I mean——" There was a pause, then Bill said, " *Ja*."

Susan said, "What did they say to you, Bill?"

"How should I know?" said Bill. "They were speaking some foreign language. Let's wait and see what happens."

What happened was that in a very few minutes a tiny speck began to swing down the thin silver thread and eventually there arrived at their feet a small red tin box.

Susan felt quite faint. She glanced at the others and was relieved to find rather anxious expressions on all their faces, which gave her courage to say, "Are we supposed to go up a sheer mountain-side in that tin can?"

"I expect it's stronger than it looks," said Charlotte in a quavering voice.

"It had better be," said Midge.

"Well, come on," Bill was saying briskly, "let's get in. They'll whizz the thing away without us if we don't look out——"

Susan thought that one of the happiest moments of her life would be to see that ghastly little tin can whizz away without them, but she was afraid that if she put such a thought into words the Carmichaels would despise her for ever.

Bill turned the handle and opened the door of the swaying contraption. "I've seen a more substantial door on a toy motor-car," Midge muttered, and they got in. There was just room for four, two on either side. Bill shut the door. There was no trim guard waiting to lock them safely into their conveyance: it swayed off into space. Susan covered her eyes with her hand as casually as she could, hoping that her intrepid cousins wouldn't notice that behind her hand her eyes were shut tight. "What happens if we stick half-way?" she murmured.

Nobody seemed to know the answer to that one.

After a minute or two Susan felt a terrible urge to open her eyes; she didn't want to, but some tremendous power was forcing her to have a look. She cautiously peered through her fingers—in front of her was the tree-clad mountain-side, at which she could look without feeling sick; encouraged by this she glanced down. Vitznau was miles away already, the lake spread out magnificently beyond it; dizzy miles below she saw fields and trees; she edged herself round a little—there was Rosendorf, peaceful in the sunshine. She quickly turned her gaze up to the mountain-side again. As long as I don't look straight down, Susan thought, I'll be all right. She glanced at the others— Charlotte and Midge were sitting with their eyes glued shut; they were holding on grimly to the sides of the car and their knuckles showed white with the force of their grip. Susan felt slightly better—until she saw Bill, who was sitting beside her and leaning half out of the window, gazing happily down into space, at which her stomach started to turn cartwheels again.

At this point the little red box headed straight for the sheer tree-covered side of the mountain. This is it! Susan thought and shut her eyes, but no crash came and she opened her eyes to find they were going up the mountain-side like a lift. They swung in under a small roof perched at the very edge of a sheer drop. They had arrived.

Two or three men were tinkering happily with the machinery of the cable-car—and Midge always afterwards maintained that she saw one of the men tie up part of the mechanism with a piece of string. One took their money and gave them tickets. They left the "station."

Sign-posts pointed to *Urmli* and *Gersau* and *Hotel*, to little paths wandering away through the woods and over meadows thick with daisies, pink clover, forget-me-not, crane's-bill, ragged robin, wild columbine, guarded by the wide wooden fences that Susan liked so much. She felt the blessed, heavenly solid earth under her—even if it was a bit high up—and began to recover. Her knees stopped wobbling and she thought that perhaps after all she wouldn't need to lie down. "Could we get some coffee somewhere?" she said. "Or lemonade. I'm parched with thirst——"

Everybody thought that something to drink was a good idea. They took the path that led to the Hotel Alpenblick. The hotel was sweet, built of brown shingles with blue shutters and crisp blue and white checked curtains fluttering at the windows. They went into the *gaststube*, as Charlotte called the dining-room, showing off a little, the others thought. It had wood-lined walls and paintings of mountain scenes here and there, and windows wide open to the mountain air, sweet with the scent of clover.

Bill and Midge ordered apple juice, Susan had coffee —she felt she needed it, for her nerves—and Charlotte ordered tea. This came in a little muslin bag attached to a glass of hot water. Charlotte put the bag into the hot water which turned a pale fawn colour, vaguely resembling tea. Charlotte said that it was absolutely ghastly.

The sight of the tea reminded Susan of the sterner purposes of their visit, so she said politely to the very pretty waitress, "Excuse me, but I wonder if you could tell me if a Fräulein Amacher is staying here by any chance?"

The waitress looked blank. "Please?" she said.

"You're too long-winded, Susie," said Charlotte. She scratched in her bag for a pencil and on the back of their bill wrote *Fräulein Amacher*. "Fräulein Amacher *ist hier, ja?*" she said, showing the name to the pretty waitress.

A curious expression came over the girl's face, then she shook her head. "*Nein,*" she said, and clearing away the cups and glasses she disappeared into the kitchen premises.

"There you are, Susie, *she* obviously doesn't know anything about Fräulein Amacher," said Charlotte.

"She didn't say she didn't know anything about

her," Susan argued, "she only said *no*. Someone here is in this thing with Fräulein Amacher or that letter wouldn't have been in the tea. Fräulein Amacher——"

"Let's not blah any more about Fräulein Amacher," Bill interrupted. "Let's go and have our picnic."

They had risen to go when an older woman appeared from the service entrance. "Good morning," she said slowly.

"Oh, good morning, madame——" said Charlotte.

"You are asking for some person?"

"Well," Charlotte shot a rather cross glance at Susan. "Well, not exactly. We only wondered if a Fräulein Amacher is staying here——"

"There is no person of that name here," said the woman. "I do not know any person of that name. I wonder why you think she might be here?" she said, looking at them strangely.

Susan, remembering the letter in the opened parcel, blushed fiery red. Guilt, confusion, embarrassment was written all over her. Charlotte rushed to her rescue. "Oh we didn't really expect to find Fräulein Amacher here we must have misunderstood we really only came for a picnic we're just going this minute for our picnic come on everybody——" she said all in one breath.

They hurriedly began gathering up bags and cardigans and packets of lunch; they said good-bye to the woman and clattered out of the *gaststube*. They rushed out of the hotel, only Susan pausing in the tiny hall to read some notices, which made Midge mutter, "Nosy as ever——" They climbed a little way farther up the hillside until they were out of sight of the hotel and flung themselves down on the flower-starred grass.

"I think we made rather a hash of *that* conversation," Midge said.

"Gosh, *yes!*" said Susan, "I could feel myself going absolutely purple with guilty blushes. But all the same," she added, "that woman Knew Something!"

Even Charlotte agreed that although *they* had behaved very stupidly, the woman had acted strangely.

I should think she's the proprietor, shouldn't you?" said Susan. If she is, her name is Weber because it was on one of the notices in the hall, that was what I stopped to look at. And Weber was the name on the envelope in the pound of tea. So there *is* a connection with Fräulein Amacher. That woman Knew Something. The name Fräulein Amacher meant something to her, all right. To the waitress too, I shouldn't wonder—now I come to think of it, *she* looked a bit queer when I asked for Fräulein Amacher; and then she rushed off to tell the other one. I expect that Fräulein Amacher *is* here, all the time, locked up in one of the bedrooms——"

Midge murmured, "Fräulein Amacher looked a pretty strong-minded old party to me. I can't see her being locked up in a bedroom against her will."

"Well, she'll be drugged, of course," said Susan, as if it was the most natural thing in the world.

"*Hon*estly, Susan——" Charlotte began.

"Old Susie must have been reading the wrong sort of books recently," said Midge. "We'd better put her on to a course of *Little Women* and nice gentle books like that and perhaps she won't have so many dotty ideas."

"She doesn't get it from books," said Bill, "she gets it out of her head, that's the trouble." But he grinned at Susan all the same, and then changed the conversation to the more interesting topic of food.

After their picnic lunch, which was of such vast proportions that Bill was the only one who managed to finish his, Charlotte took out her sketching things, Midge stretched out on the grass, put a sun hat over her face and went to sleep. The sun was hot and comforting on them, but was tempered by the cool mountain air which seemed to have a breath of the high snows in it.

Susan glanced at the sleeping Midge and at Charlotte, absorbed in her flowers. "Bill," she whispered, "What about a bit of an explore?" She could usually count on Bill, she thought.

Bill wiped his orange-stained fingers on the seat of his khaki shorts. "Good idea," he said. "Don't you want that chocolate?" he added.

"I don't at the moment, but I shall later," said Susan, putting her chocolate and packet of biscuits into her bag. They both got up and climbed through the wooden fence on to the path again.

"Which way?" Bill asked.

Susan made a warning jerk of her head in Charlotte's direction then drew Bill farther down the path. "I didn't want Charlotte to hear," she said, "for you know what a fuss she makes about everything, but the thing is, Bill, I'm not a bit satisfied that poor old Fräulein Amacher isn't tucked away somewhere in the hotel here. We *know* that there's a connection because of the letter in the tea—I jolly well wish now that I'd just opened it and not listened to Charlotte— and you must admit that it was perfectly obvious to the meanest intelligence——"

"Charlotte's," Bill put in.

"Well, yes, even to Charlotte's, whose intelligence isn't exactly mean, would you say, only different from ours?—it was obvious even to Charlotte that the hotel proprietor *did* know Fräulein Amacher although she pretended not to——"

"So?" Bill prompted.

"So it must be guilty knowledge or she would have said yes, how is my old pal Fräulein Amacher, when we asked, so——"

"So?" Bill prompted again.

"So I think we should have a quiz round the hotel," Susan said, "when we're here——"

Bill didn't object to this idea. All that worried him was the method. Charlotte would *kill* them if they did anything silly. "How?" he asked.

"Well," said Susan, "we can ask to see the bedrooms. That's quite a usual thing for people to do, Mummy's always doing it, she adores seeing over hotels. We could say that we'd like to come and stay here because we've taken such a fancy to the place—and that's perfectly true——"

"You can say that again," said Bill. "It's a jolly nice little hotel——"

"I'd like it better if it was a *little* bit back from the edge of the precipice and not perched right above a sheer drop," Susan admitted.

"But Susan," Bill went on, "they're not likely to show us the room where Fräulein Amacher is lying bound and gagged."

"Of course not," said Susan, "but when we get upstairs I thought that you could fall downstairs and cause a diversion and I'll have a quick look round——"

This seemed feasible enough to Bill except for the bit about falling downstairs. "You could fall downstairs," he suggested, "and *I'll* look round——"

"You don't actually have to fall downstairs," said Susan, "you could faint."

"Faint!" said Bill scornfully. "Boys don't faint!"

"Well, you can think of something," said Susan.

They decided that the young and pretty waitress would be a better one to tackle than the proprietor, but as luck would have it they bumped straight into the proprietor as they were creeping cautiously from the little hall to the *gaststube* and which now smelt deliciously of the luncheon that had just been served and cleared away. When the proprietor appeared Susan jumped guiltily, but rushed quickly into her request before the woman could begin to wonder why they were sneaking round her hotel in this suspicious fashion. To their intense surprise she agreed at once to their suggestion. "But of course I let you see the bedrooms," she said, "naturally, most are filled up, but I have one or two empty and I show you. Come——" She led the way upstairs.

She plied them with questions all the time—their names, where they were staying, when they had seen their friend Fräulein Amacher, and again what had made them think that she might be there. Susan answered the other questions readily enough and evaded the ones about Fräulein Amacher. Far from her pumping the hotel proprietor, she realised, she was being pumped herself, which probably explained the proprietor's willingness to show them round the hotel at all. This didn't make Fräulein Amacher's concealment in the actual hotel seem very likely, therefore, but Susan wanted to make sure so she felt that she should go on with the search if possible. But here they were, a very nice room, wood-panelled, on the first floor inspected, just about to mount to the second floor and Bill hadn't fainted or fallen downstairs or *anything*! Really, if Bill couldn't think up a bright idea to get this *frau* out of the way, it hadn't been much use bringing him.

"Now we go upstairs," the *frau* was saying. But Bill had stopped with his head on one side, listening.

"What was that?" he said.

The *frau* stopped too. "I heard nothing," she said.

"*Didn't* you?" said Bill. "A terrific crash and then a scream—you heard it, Susan, didn't you?"

"Well, I heard *some*thing," said Susan, crossing her fingers. "More like terrible moans than screams, didn't you think?"

The *frau* glanced at her sharply and they all stood listening. There wasn't a sound.

"There!" exclaimed Bill. "Didn't you hear *that*, Frau er—um——? A scream from downstairs?"

The *frau* turned and ran downstairs, Susan ran upstairs and Bill sat down on the bottom step. He felt rather pleased with himself and was just congratulating himself on his strong powers of suggestion when from the floor above came a scream that owed nothing to the powers of suggestion. A door banged, Susan came flying downstairs and reached Bill just as the *frau* came upstairs. Scream after scream rent the air, doors opened and people looked out, the hotel proprietor ran upstairs, there was a babble of talk in Swiss and the screams stopped.

Bill looked at Susan. "Is this your doing?" he asked.

Susan stirred uncomfortably. "Well, I'm afraid so," she admitted. "Actually it was ghastly—I tried one or two doors and of course they were locked, I never thought of that, did you?"—and then this one was open and I peeped in and saw an ancient grey head on the pillow! I was thrilled, I was sure it was Fräulein Amacher, lying in a drugged sleep! But her face was hidden by the *duvet*, you know the way they billow, so I tiptoed round the bed until I could see her face and of course it wasn't Fräulein Amacher and she wasn't even asleep, just lying there with her mouth open staring at me—and then she began to scream and I ran——"

Frau Weber came downstairs, looking harassed. "Poor Fräulein Wasserman!" she said. "She is having a little sleep after lunch, what you call forty vinks, and then she is having a bad dream—she is having a very good appetite for so old a person and is eating a good lunch you understand—she is telling me a horrible creature with the eyes that stare and vild black hair all over its head like Struwwelpeter is coming into her room and is going to strangle her——"

Bill glanced at Susan who looked affronted.

"—I go downstairs now and find her a something to soothe the nerves. You excuse?"

"Of *course*, Frau er—um," Susan said. "Thank you *very* much for showing us the hotel. We'll go and join the others now, we're having a picnic in a field, and we'll bring my aunt here one day to see your hotel, it's so sweet——"

Frau Weber led the way downstairs. When Bill and Susan left her she was wondering a little anxiously if she were going deaf? Strange how the boy had heard the screams. . . .

Susan and Bill walked up the path. Over on their left lay a shed from which came the sound of a high-pitched whine. "I realise now," Susan said, "that it might not be very practical to keep Fräulein Amacher shut up at the hotel. D'you think she could be imprisoned somewhere else—in that shed, f'r instance?" She nodded towards it.

"Don't be an ass, that's a cow-shed."

"I never heard cows making a noise like that."

"Well of course not, *that* noise is a circular saw. Let's go and have a look——"

In the open shed two men were working the saw; huge trees were being sawn up into logs in a few seconds. Behind was the cow-shed; every now and then came the sweet tinkle of a cow-bell and the sound of the beasts as they moved about in their stalls. Susan walked over to the half-door and looked in; the shed was almost dark, exceedingly dirty, which was rather odd since the Swiss were so fanatically clean in every other way, and the cows' tails were tied up to the ceiling. As her eyes became accustomed to the gloom, she realised that a small boy was staring at her. He was about nine, she supposed, or less, with a thatch of dark hair and big dark eyes and his face seemed vaguely familiar to Susan although she couldn't place it. She remembered the chocolate left over from lunch. She took it out of her bag and offered it to the boy. "Go on," she said, "take it. You like chocolate?"

A wide beam suddenly lighted the child's face. "*Danke*," he said, and snatching the chocolate he disappeared among the cows.

"Funny little boy," said Susan, as she went up the path with Bill. "Can't help feeling I've seen him before somewhere——"

"In Rosendorf, probably," said Bill.

" 'Mm. Probably," said Susan.

Susan did her best to persuade everybody to walk down the mountain instead of taking the red tin can. Charlotte hesitated, obviously tempted, but Midge was too lazy and Bill said, "And miss the cable-car? Oh gosh *no*," and even Susan, remembering in her frugal way that they had taken return tickets, thought that perhaps going down might be better than coming up.

It wasn't. It was a thousand times worse. When their conveyance came up, there was a man and an Alsatian dog in it and a huge length of drain-pipe was tied to the roof. The dog jumped out non-chalantly, followed by the man, who then leant dizzily over space and untied his drainpipe. For perhaps the first time in her life Susan didn't offer to help. But somehow the sight of the dog encouraged her. Well if a *dog* can do it—she thought, and stepped into the car which rocked violently, feeling quite brave. This feeling disappeared immediately as the car dropped rapidly down the cliff face into space. She looked down once and was so appalled at the distance they were from the ground that she closed her eyes quickly as a shudder of absolute terror went through her. Midge said plaintively that she had left her tummy up at Wissifluh and Bill said, "Talking about tummies, I could eat those biscuits that you left at lunch-time, Susie. I mean, we get gorgeous food in this place but I'm jolly hungry by dinner. Don't forget we have no tea——"

"Tea!" exclaimed Susan, opening her eyes and quite forgetting in her excitement her horror of heights, "Now I know why that little boy's face was familiar! It was his photo on the passport that was hidden in the tea!"

All the way back from Vitznau to Rosendorf, Susan worried away at the Mystery of the Black-haired Boy, as she called it. Charlotte was so bored with the whole affair that she wouldn't even stay beside Susan on the boat, but drifted away by herself. Midge kept repeating in reply to Susan's unanswerable questions that there did seem to be some sort of mystery, but that frankly she didn't see what it had to do with them: and Bill, rather put off Susan's interfering ways by the screaming lady at Wissifluh, kept trying to divert Susan's thoughts into other channels by a change of subject. "Nearly home now," he said brightly at one of the few lulls in Susan's monologue, "I should think we'd have time for a swim before dinner—there's the first chalet in Rosendorf, that pretty one—look, Susan, someone is being carried inside—the people must have arrived, you remember we saw the beds and *duvets* being aired yesterday——"

Susan, intent on her black-haired boy, ignored him; but as a matter of fact she should have paid more attention to his last remarks, for the real clue to the mystery of Fräulein Amacher's disappearance was before her eyes.

CHAPTER SIX

FINDING FRÄULEIN AMACHER

NEXT MORNING Aunt Lucy couldn't figure out why the three girls were so lukewarm about her plan for the day, which was to go to the Joch Pass. "I've been looking it up in one of Bill's leaflets," she said. "We take the boat to Stansstad, then a mountain railway up to Engelberg, then the funicular to Gerschni Alp, then the cable railway to a little lake called Trübsee, then a chair-lift to the Joch Pass——"

"Cable-railway," said Midge in a faint voice.

"Chair-lift," said Susan in an even fainter voice.

"What's that?" said Bill.

"Well, I've never been on one," said Aunt Lucy, "but it's a chair that takes you up the mountain. Skiers use them a lot in winter, they are like a cable-car, I suppose really, only a chair——"

"Just a chair?" asked Susan. "Hanging in mid-air? No glass round you? Swinging up the mountain?"

"I imagine so, yes," said Aunt Lucy.

There was a pause.

"We had rather fancied a lazy day just here in Rosendorf," said Charlotte, elaborately casual. "Swimming in the lake, you know, p'raps taking a boat out——"

"After all," said Susan, equally casual, "we are here for a month. We could go to the Joch Pass *any* day——"

89

"Just as you like," said Aunt Lucy. "Then I'll have a lazy day too. I'll have a lovely morning pottering round the shops and perhaps I'll get my postcards sent off to-day instead of waiting for the last day of the holidays as I usually do——"

"And I shall lie on my back in the sun in the garden," said Uncle Charles, "thinking about my locum rushing round my patients. Did you know that there is a monument to Mark Twain in the garden?"

"Mark Twain?" asked Charlotte. "The man who wrote *Tom Sawyer*? Did he stay here?"

"Apparently," said Uncle Charles. "He said this was the most beautiful place in the world or words to that effect."

"He was right too," said Susan, gazing soulfully across the lake to Pilatus, veiled, as it so often was, in a thin trail of mist.

Only Bill was rather disappointed because of missing the chair-lift, but Midge promised that they would take a boat out on the lake and that he could row all the time, at which, extraordinary as it seemed to her, he cheered up again.

When Bill and the girls were rowing gently up the lake towards Vitznau, Susan said, "You know it wasn't that I didn't want to go to this Joch Pass or whatever it's called, it sounded *very* interesting, didn't you think——?"

"Ghastly," said Midge. "Dangling over precipices in a chair!"

"Oh well, of course it is rather nice to be at ground level again," said Susan airily, "but the real reason I didn't particularly want to go to-day was that I thought we ought to be getting on with all those problems. We have two mysteries to deal with, don't forget——"

"Oh help," said Midge, "are we going over all this again?"

"Well we didn't reach any conclusions," said Susan. "There's a mystery about Fräulein Amacher, disappearing like that, nobody can deny *that*. And there's a mystery about that boy up at Wissifluh and Frau Weber who pretended she didn't know anything about Fräulein Amacher and all the time she's jolly well mixed up in that pound of tea we brought over——"

Midge said, "Very scratchy being mixed up in a pound of tea," and Susan sprinkled some drops of lake water on her from her oar and Bill complained that Susan wasn't keeping time.

"Susan never does keep time," said Charlotte rather morosely, from the bow where she was watching out for steamers. "She's always racing ahead of everybody on some crack-brained wild-goose chase or other——"

Susan said she thought that was rather a rude thing to say and didn't Charlotte *want* to rescue Fräulein Amacher who had, after all, been jolly nice to them, asking them to tea and everything?

Charlotte said shortly that in her opinion Fräulein Amacher didn't need any rescuing, and as for the other business about the small boy at Wissifluh, she didn't see what it had to do with them and couldn't Susan even give a piece of chocolate to a small boy she met in a cow-shed without wanting to interfere in his life?"

"*Interfere?*" said Susan. "*Me?*"

And that made everybody laugh so much that unfortunately nobody paid any attention to the steering and they ran aground—almost into the wall that surrounded the pretty chalet in the beautiful gardens.

Bill told them all to get out as the boat would then probably float again without the girls' weight, and Susan obligingly floundered out. She misjudged her jump however and landed in the water. Charlotte jumped out and got her feet a bit wet too; Midge said that she wasn't going to fall in the lake for anybody and couldn't Susan and Charlotte push the boat off seeing they were wet anyway?

"We're not as wet as all that," said Charlotte. "Come on, get out."

Midge got out and went and sat with her back against the chalet wall until the navigators should have finished arguing. Then Bill managed to push off with his oar and manœuvred the boat alongside a convenient jetty beside the wall. Susan put her sandals in the sun to dry and joined Midge against the wall in the shade of an overhanging tree. She had made the interesting discovery that her hands were beginning to blister and if Midge and Charlotte weren't prepared to take over the rowing for a bit, she said, she thought she ought to have a rest.

"Yes do let poor Susan have a rest," said Midge. "It's nice and cool here in the shade."

Charlotte sat against the wall and Bill was just tying up the boat when the sound of voices came from over the wall. "I wonder what kind of people own this chalet—it's a heavenly place——" Susan was beginning when suddenly the rumble of talk was interrupted by a voice saying sharply in English, "Never! Never! You will never make me do that, not for all your millions, not for all the money in the world!" The answering voices died away.

Susan and the Carmichaels stared at each other in silence. At last Susan whispered, "That was Fräulein Amacher's voice!"

Nobody could deny it. There was no mistaking Fräulein Amacher's clear, high decisive tones.

Susan had gone quite pale. "I t-t-told you!" she whispered, stuttering a little in her excitement. "I told you something had happened to her! And now you see! She's being held a prisoner here and they want her to do something and she won't do it!" Suddenly a memory struck her. "Yesterday!" she said. "Bill! You remember! You were talking about it! We saw somebody being carried into this house! I bet that was poor old Fräulein Amacher bound and gagged and helpless!"

"She's not gagged now," Midge whispered, reasonably enough.

"No, she isn't, but for how long will she be free to speak if she defies the gang like this?" said Susan. She glanced over her shoulder up at the wall. "I'm going to have a look——"

The wall which encircled the garden and which a little farther from where they were sitting went straight down into the lake, was not so high at this point and seemed easy enough to climb. Susan thrust her feet into her wet sandals and climbed up. She clung, spread-eagled, to the wall. Very cautiously she raised her head over the top. There was the sound of a voice shouting angrily, Susan hurriedly began to climb down, missed her footing and fell in a heap on the grass. A man's head appeared over the edge of the wall. He began shouting again and making violent signs to them to remove themselves.

"Goodness, he's cross," muttered Charlotte. "All because Susie poked her head over the wall!" She said to the man coldly, "We weren't doing any harm, we were only——"

At the sound of the English speech the man calmed down considerably. "Excuse please," he mumbled in English, "I not know you are English visitors." Then his temper seemed to get the better of him again and he went on, "But you must understand that you are on private ground. Please to go——"

Putting on a great show of offended dignity, the girls and Bill re-embarked in their dinghy and pushed off. The man, who seemed to be in some sort of uniform, perhaps a chauffeur's, stood and watched them go.

"Honestly," said Charlotte when they were out of earshot, "ordering us off like that! Such cheek!"

"Well they can't have stray tourists poking their noses in if they're keeping poor old Fräulein Amacher a prisoner there——" began Susan.

"Who can't?" Midge asked.

"The Gang, of course!" said Susan. Her cheeks were bright red and her dark eyes sparkled with excitement. Being ordered off the premises like this was complete confirmation of her suspicions and theories. "All this makes me think more and more that Fräulein Amacher is up to her neck in some underground movement, and unfortunately the rival gang have got her. They're probably torturing her to give away information at this very moment!"

Charlotte said in an exaggeratedly dramatic voice, "Gangs! Torture!"

Susan grinned. "Och, you can jeer," she said, "but you've got to admit that Fräulein Amacher is *there*! And she must be there against her will or she would have turned up at the Chalet du Lac long ago. It's only five minutes' walk from that chalet to the hotel and she has been gone two days. She's a prisoner, all right——"

"We must rescue her," said Bill.

"Now?" asked Midge.

"How?" asked Charlotte.

"Not now, of course not," said Susan. "That cheeky man is still watching us. At night, I should say. And I don't know *how*. We'll need to think——"

They thought all day and produced lots of schemes— at least Susan and Bill produced the schemes and Charlotte and Midge poured cold water on them. In the end they could think of nothing better than breaching the chalet's defences by sea as Bill called it, in other words climbing in by the lake wall and having a good snoop round. Susan suggested that after dinner, when Aunt Lucy and Uncle Charles had gone into the village to have coffee at the Confiserie Hofmann would be the best time.

There were various objections to this, the main one being that Aunt Lucy would be sure to wonder why the family didn't want to go with her and Uncle Charles that night when they had gone every other night and indeed more or less made a scene at any suggestion of their staying behind. But as it happened it was Aunt Lucy who made everything simple for the rescue-party. There was to be a concert in one of the hotels, given by the Rosendorf orchestra, and Aunt Lucy herself suggested that it would be too late for Bill. She was quite touched when the whole family insisted on staying at home to keep Bill company.

It was a dark night when the girls and Bill went down to the hotel landing-stage and untied the dinghy, but the gleam of the rising moon could be seen behind the mountains. The lights of faraway chalets twinkled on the heights, Wissifluh was a bright glow as usual and the pencil of light which was the lift up the mountain called the Burgenstock, opposite Rosendorf, looked strange and spectral across the lake.

" We mustn't land," Susan was organising the rescue-party as they rowed up the lake, " we'd make too much noise. I suggest that we climb the wall from the boat——"

"And then the boat drifts away and we're nicely marooned in the Gang's garden?" said Charlotte.

"Or," said Midge, "as seems more likely, we annoy some law-abiding Swiss householders and have to *walk* back to the hotel." This was apparently the worst fate that could befall Midge.

"We can't all go swarming into these people's garden," said Charlotte. "I vote that Susan goes first——"

"I second that. And if she doesn't come back," said Midge with relish, "it's no great loss anyway."

"How unkind you are to me!" said Susan plaintively. "Can Bill come with me?"

"Good gracious no," said Midge, "we need him to look after the boat——"

They were now approaching the walls round the chalet, which they could just make out, a darker mass, against the faintly luminous waters of the lake. "Now, is it all quite clear what we have to do?" said Susan bossily.

"It's quite clear what *we* have to do," said Midge. "Nothing. The thing is, are you quite clear about what you have to do?"

"All I have to do," said Susan, "is climb into the garden and have a good look round while you wait for me below. You won't forget," she added, "that you're my only way of escape?"

Charlotte, whose misgivings about the whole enterprise had been gradually increasing, said anxiously, "Susan, you will take care, won't you?"

"Yes, do, Susie," said Midge. "At the first sign of revolvers, knives, hand-grenades, tommy-guns et cetera, run like a rabbit——"

Susan said severely, "You don't seem to be taking this rescue operation very seriously, Midge——"

"It's time you all shut up," Bill said, "you know how voices carry across water."

Everybody fell silent. Bill took over both oars and manœuvred the boat under the walls of the chalet embankment. But what Susan had not bargained for was the difficulty of climbing a wall from a gently heaving boat. Before Bill could even whisper "Trim the boat!" she had tried to stand on the gunwale and had nearly sent them all to the bottom of the lake. She had a few angry remarks hissed at her, but she did better on her next attempt. Not that she managed to climb the wall, but at least she didn't capsise the boat. She tried again; then she put her mouth to Bill's ear and whispered, "Every time I try to get a hand-hold on the wall the boat drifts away, I'm stretched out like a piece of elastic and I nearly fall in. Can't you do something?"

"We really need grappling-irons," Bill whispered back, but after a struggle he managed to get a grip on the stones and to keep the boat steady enough for Susan to find foot-and hand-holds on the wall.

"Okay now," she breathed, and disappeared upwards over the wall.

For what seemed like hours the three in the boat sat silently. Suddenly there was a tremendous splash— and then voices called out in Swiss and people shouted and after a little, a pencil of light began moving along the wall towards the boat.

"Bill!" whispered Charlotte urgently. "Someone's coming with a torch! Better row away a bit!"

Bill pushed off with one oar, and with as little sound as possible rowed until he judged the boat to be out of range of the searching torch. "We'll stay here until the excitement has died down," he whispered. "What *has* that dotty idiot been up to?"

The dotty idiot meantime was behind a tree, soaked to the skin and shivering with cold and terror. It was *extremely* bad luck, she felt, that before she had even got the length of the lighted windows she should step into space and find herself sinking rapidly to the bottom of a deep pool of water. Really, she thought, what a thing to have in the middle of a garden! And it wasn't until she had tried without success to clamber out of this death-trap that she realised that she had fallen into a swimming-pool. The Gang, to crown all, were of course thoroughly roused—that splash, she thought, could have been heard at Lucerne— she could hear them shouting and rushing about the place. Nor could she get out of the pool, hampered as she was by her water-logged clothing. She was working her way round the edge, hoping to come to some steps, when she saw a light wavering across the garden. Oh *help*, she thought, someone's coming with a torch! She took a deep breath and slowly sank once more beneath the surface of the water. Above her, distorted by the wavering water, she saw a light flashing this way and that. When her bursting lungs could stand no more, she surfaced again—if the Gang were still there it was just too bad—she'd rather be captured than drowned. However, the pool was again in darkness; the flickering torch was moving in the direction of the lake-wall. At last she found some steps and thankfully climbed out. She squelched soggily behind a tree and waited. If the person with the torch should turn and come back she would be discovered and dragged before the Gang! Even if no one spotted her, there was no hope of her finding out anything about Fräulein Amacher to-night, the Gang would be on the alert now. All she could do, she thought, was consider her own skin, circle round behind the person with the torch and make her escape.

Overhanging trees made it very dark in the garden; but by now her eyes were more accustomed to the gloom. She crept across grass to the wall and cautiously felt her way along it, behind the searcher, until she reached the spot below which the boat was waiting and which she had marked with a big stone. She didn't dare call to Bill and the others below. Hoping that any sound she made would be covered by the noise of the searcher's own movements she climbed over the wall. "Hey!" she whispered as loudly as she dared, "Trim the boat! Here I come!" She slithered down, painfully grazing her hands and knees, straight down into the dark waters of the lake. Oh gosh, she thought, not again!

Susan came to the surface gasping and choking. Gang or no Gang she had no intention of drowning. "*Help!*" she yelled and dog-paddled violently.

In the boat Bill exclaimed, "That's Susan's voice!"

"Was that splash Susan?" Charlotte said in wonder. "What on *earth* is she playing at, jumping in the lake?"

"We'd better go and see," said Bill and rowed vigorously in the direction of the splash.

He reached Susan at the same moment as the person with the torch located her. The torch shone down on a dripping Susan, who was hanging on to the boat and pushing the wet hair out of her eyes and assuring the others, who weren't asking her, that she was perfectly all right and the water wasn't a *bit* cold, much warmer than she expected and a jolly lot warmer than it was during the day sometimes, but that she would like to know what *they* thought they were doing, moving the boat just when she wanted to get into it?

As the beam of light found them, they all looked up. "Charlotte! Midge! Bill! *Susan!*" said an astounded voice, the voice of Fräulein Amacher— Fräulein Amacher, who was not lying drugged and gagged and bound in some dungeon cell but walking about with a torch!

The whole situation, they felt, definitely wanted some straightening out, but Charlotte thought that sitting in a boat, with Susan hanging on like a drowned rat, wasn't the place to do it. Fräulein Amacher told them to get the boat into the jetty and guided them with her torch. She was in favour of taking Susan up to the house immediately to get dry things, but the idea of walking into a house full of strangers— and Swiss strangers at that—in her present bedraggled condition, daunted even Susan.

"Then you must run straight back to the hotel and have a bath and go straight to bed," said Fräulein Amacher.

Susan didn't like to mention that baths cost five shillings extra and that she had no intention of wasting five shillings on a bath, but she made an agreeing sort of noise. "But Fräulein Amacher," she went on, "what about you? Are you all right?"

"*I?* I am all right. I did not fall into the lake," said Fräulein Amacher in rather a schoolmistressy way.

"Yes, I *know*," said Susan, "but are you safe?"

"*Safe?*" said Fräulein Amacher.

Goodness she's dense, thought Susan. "Yes, safe," she repeated in a loud clear voice, for perhaps Fräulein Amacher's English wasn't as good as everybody thought. "We thought that you were in some danger. That's why we came to look for you——"

"You were looking for me?" said Fräulein Amacher. "But you knew I was here——"

Gosh, thought Susan, grown-ups! They really are the end. "Well, no, Fräulein Amacher," she said diffidently, not liking to contradict, "truly we didn't know you were here. All we knew was that you had disappeared——"

"I? Disappeared?" Fräulein Amacher seemed to be able only to repeat every word that Susan said. "But I had not disappeared. I came here rather unexpectedly, I admit, but I asked my neighbour, Frau Tannenbaum, to telephone to the Chalet du Lac and tell them I am here and to ask *you* to come and see me——"

"Well, I just don't understand it," Susan said helplessly, "because it was Frau Tannenbaum who told us that you had gone away and that she didn't know where you were and offered to keep the parcel of tea for you!"

Fräulein Amacher made a curious small sound, almost a gasp, Susan would have said. "Did you give her the parcel?" she asked sharply.

"No," said Susan virtuously, "we refused, politely of course. We said we'd rather give it to you direct——"

"Good girl," said Fräulein Amacher. "At least," she went on, more easily, "I do not think it would have mattered, but she seems a very queer person and it is better that I have little to do with her——"

Susan wasn't deceived. She knew that it was vitally important to Fräulein Amacher that the famous pound of tea should on no account be given to anyone but herself, and Susan waited confidently for Fräulein Amacher to give them an explanation of all these goings-on. But no explanation was forthcoming. Fräulein Amacher said briskly, "There is some mystery here, but we must wait until to-morrow to solve it. Now, you must all run to the hotel immediately or Susan will die of the cold. To-morrow you will come and take your boat——"

Ugh, thought Midge disgustedly, I *knew* this escapade would end in my having to walk home. . . .

They were extremely thankful, not for the first time, that their rooms were in the seclusion of the chalet, for Susan was leaving awkward little pools of water at every step.

"We'd better hurry up and get you into bed before Aunt Lucy sees you," said Charlotte as they went upstairs.

"I won't be sorry to get into bed," said Susan. "I'm jolly tired after all that excitement——"

"Not to mention two swims," murmured Midge.

But when they reached the girls' room they could hardly see the bed for the stuff—dresses, shoes, underwear, books—that were tossed about the room.

"Well *hon*estly, Susan," said Charlotte, "you might have tidied your room before you went out——"

"You don't think *I* did that?" indignantly demanded Susan.

Midge and Bill craned their necks over the shoulders of Charlotte and Susan to look into the room.

"Crumbs!" said Bill. "You lucky things, you've had a burglar!"

Bill needn't have envied the girls' burglar; he had had one too, everybody had had one, all the rooms in the chalet had been turned upside down. Frau Stocker, summoned by Bill while Susan hastily put on dry clothes, was dreadfully upset. But the funny thing was that nothing seemed to be missing; until, after Frau Stocker had gone, she said, to talk to the police, Midge suddenly said, "*Susan!* Fräulein Amacher's pound of tea!"

Susan looked at her blankly. "Is *that* what the burglar came for?"

"Well you said yourself that someone seemed mighty anxious to get hold of it. Oh dear, and now it's gone!"

"Gone?" said Susan. "What d'you mean, gone?"

Susan's duckings had apparently affected her brain, Midge thought. "Well, it's not here, is it?" she said impatiently.

"I should think not," said Susan. "You don't think I was going to leave a valuable parcel—goodness, it's so valuable to someone that they nearly pushed me under a car to get it——"

"Susan," said Charlotte, "WHERE IS IT?"

"In the hotel safe," said Susan calmly.

CHAPTER SEVEN

NEW FRIENDS AND OLD ENEMIES

FRÄULEIN AMACHER was at the hotel to see them before breakfast. She and Susan and Charlotte and Bill sat in the garden and talked: Midge was still in bed. Discussing it the night before, Susan had been scarcely able to believe that their whole explanation of the situation had been imagination—goodness, they had practically *seen* Fräulein Amacher being carried into that mystery house! They had heard her very vehemently refusing to fall in with the plans of the Gang—how was Fräulein Amacher going to explain all that?

She explained it all very easily. She was staying at the chalet, which was called See Perle, with her friends Herr Schriber and his daughter Lise to whom she had once been governess. Six months before Lise, who was now eighteen, had most unfortunately contracted polio, from which she had mercifully recovered, but which had left her lame. "Not a helpless cripple, you understand," said Fräulein Amacher, "but Lise will not try to walk. She was formerly a very pretty girl, so graceful and elegant, and she says that she will not be seen by people hobbling about, she would rather not walk at all! And the sad thing is that the more she exercises and uses her leg the better it will become—it will never be quite right, but it will improve, but nothing will induce her to walk, except in her bedroom perhaps, or in the garden when she is quite, quite alone—— Well, three days ago her father brought her from Zürich to the chalet here for a holiday, and he has asked me to come to live with them again for a little to be a companion to Lise and to see if I can persuade her to stop this silliness about her limp and live a normal life—her father spoils her, I am afraid, but it is natural because she has no mother, and now this horrible illness——" Fräulein Amacher glanced round at her audience, who were listening with rapt attention. "So now you understand why I had to make my plans very quickly and I leave my flat very quickly! But now you must tell me why you think I was in danger?"

Susan and the others looked extremely uncomfortable and shuffled their feet. Susan blushed.

Fräulein Amacher looked at them gravely, although there was a twinkle in those alert grey eyes of hers. "You are shy to speak," she said, "as the English always are when they have done something brave. Although I was in no danger you thought that I was and you were coming to help me. I must thank you for that——"

"To give Susan her due, Fräulein Amacher," said Charlotte, "the rest of us weren't a bit keen, it was Susan who was determined to rescue you."

Susan was feeling a complete fool. "I'm afraid, Fräulein Amacher," she confessed, "I wasn't really being brave at all I was just being nosy. I'm always barging into other people's affairs and the others get frightfully fed up with me. But we—I—really

did think that you had been kidnapped or something—
I was sure that you wouldn't just go off without a
word to the hotel, there was the correspondence for
one thing——" and then she recounted the chain of
"evidence" which had led her to her quite erroneous
conclusions—the queer behaviour of Frau Tannenbaum, Fräulein Amacher's vigorous protests in the
chalet garden, the figure they had seen being carried
into the chalet, the surly chauffeur who had ordered
them off. It sounded rather thin, even to herself,
Susan had to admit, but then the others wouldn't let
her mention the really alarming or puzzling things,
like the man in the Kapellgasse who, in spite of all
that the others could say, *did* try to grab the parcel,
and the ransacking of the rooms the night before.
Nor did she mention the fact that she had opened the
parcel nor the black-haired boy at Wissifluh.

Fräulein Amacher was laughing. "The behaviour
of Frau Tannenbaum I cannot explain," she said.
"I did not know that she is such a lover of tea that she
must steal my precious parcel! But of course the
person being carried into the chalet was Lise, and
when you heard me protesting so loudly in the garden
I was refusing to push Lise through Rosendorf in a
chair—what you call, I think, a Bathroom chair——"

"Not a *Bathroom* chair, Fräulein Amacher," Susan
kindly explained, "a *Bath* chair—it's called after a
town and has nothing to do with a bath——"

"So?" said Fräulein Amacher. "I have always said
that English is a strange language! But push Lise in a
Bath chair I shall not! Johann must do that if Lise
insists. Johann is the chauffeur, he is not a bad fellow

but Lise has ordered him to keep strangers from coming near—she is so needlessly sensitive about herself. I tell her that no one is looking at her, but as yet she will not believe me. She thinks the whole world is staring at her and her lame leg——"

Susan felt pretty stupid at Fräulein Amacher's matter of fact explanations of all her lurid imaginings; and they were all much touched by the sad tale of Lise. They gladly accepted Fräulein Amacher's invitation to come and meet her and cheer her up; and then Susan ran to the office and got the parcel and at *last* handed over to Fräulein Amacher the famous pound of tea.

It wasn't until much later that it dawned on her that Fräulein Amacher, with all her explanations, hadn't explained a word about the passport in the tea nor about the boy at Wissifluh; but by that time gangs, secret agents, passports, mysteries, black-haired boys, all were forgotten, swallowed up in the much more interesting problem of what she was going to do about Lise.

If only she could make Lise walk again! That would be something much more wonderful than penny-dreadful gangs and rubbish like that! Even when Midge said, and what about the underground movement that Fräulein Amacher belongs to, Susan said airily that she had been slightly off the beam there, that now she was quite sure that there was some simple explanation for the passport in the tea and the black-haired boy at Wissifluh, and if Fräulein Amacher hadn't mentioned either, that was her business not Susan's, after all. Her cousins gaped at her when

she came out with these views. If Susan got the length
of admitting that Fräulein Amacher's affairs weren't
her business then things were certainly looking up.
Of course on the other hand she seemed to be pretty
well determined on interfering in Lise's affairs; even
before she met the unfortunate girl she had it all
worked out. "When I think of her lying there," she
said, "beautiful and helpless——!"

Charlotte interrupted. "Did I say we should put
Susan on to a course of *Little Women*?"

" 'Mm," said Midge, "*that* was a mistake. Lise is all
lined up already for the rôle of Beth, the sweet and
loving and patient invalid——"

"Gosh, yes," said Susan, her eyes shining. "Of
course it will be wonderful when I get her on her
feet, but can't you just see her, frail and lovely and an
inspiration to everybody with her uncomplaining
courage?"

Everybody could see this picture quite clearly, so
that it was a shock that when they first saw Lise she
should be throwing things at a maid and shouting.

"Behave yourself, Lise," said Fräulein Amacher
severely, as she led Susan and the Carmichaels to where
Lise was lying in the garden under the shade of a tree.

"She is an idiot," said Lise. "She brings me books
that I have read ten thousand times——"

Fräulein Amacher introduced everybody to everybody else. Herr Schriber was a fat, gentle-looking
little man and not at all Susan's idea of a wealthy
industrialist. Lise was beautiful. Her fair hair lay
curled close to her lovely little head; her eyes, Susan
was sure, were as blue as the gentians on her native

mountains. She lay on a long garden chair, a light rug over her legs. Beside her stood a table covered with fruit, chocolates, books and magazines. She could look over the low wall and away up the lake to the glorious mountains; behind her was the very large, very grand swimming-pool, sparkling blue and inviting in the sunshine, into which Susan had plunged uninvited. Whenever she wanted anything her father rushed to get it for her, if she dropped a handkerchief on the grass the man in uniform who had shouted at Susan and the Carmichaels appeared from nowhere and picked it up. A maid, in sober black with the usual pretty little snow-white apron in *broderie anglaise*, hovered in the background, presumably to be ready in case Lise felt like throwing things at her again. Only Fräulein Amacher seemed out of place in this throng of courtiers, for occasionally her alert glance seemed to say that if she had her way she would send the whole lot packing and order Miss Lise to get up and fetch and carry for herself.

Susan and Midge and Charlotte disposed themselves around Lise on the grass. Bill wandered off and was soon deep in conversation with Johann the disagreeable chauffeur who could not have been so disagreeable after all because before long he had provided Bill with a fishing-rod and was teaching him to fish over the wall in a quiet corner. Herr Schriber and Fräulein Amacher went into the house and the girls talked. Lise spoke English very well, which was not surprising in a pupil of Fräulein Amacher's, and she knew London well—at least she knew places like the Ritz and the Savoy which were just grand names to Susan and

Midge and Charlotte. Charlotte and Lise did most of the talking; Midge went to sleep, or seemed to, and Susan was very subdued and made no attempt to alter Lise's life, not at least at this stage. She had a faint try when Lise suggested a swim. " Are you swimming too?" she asked.

"No," said Lise.

" Oh *do*," said Susan brightly. " It would be fun——"

" What would be *fun*, as you call it?" she asked. " Watching me floundering about like a fish that is half-dead?"

" No, of *course* not!" cried Susan, blushing and embarrassed. " Just all of us swimming together would be fun was all I meant. And actually," she hurried on, " I thought that swimming was one of the things that people who had had polio could do——"

" I can swim very well indeed," said Lise. " But I prefer to swim in private."

" But don't you think——" Susan began, when both Charlotte and Midge, who can't have been sleeping after all, began to speak very loudly and both together and drowned whatever tactless interfering remarks that Susan was about to make. Later, when on their way back to the Chalet du Lac for lunch, Midge brought up the subject again.

" I can't see your bossy, interfering ways having much effect on that girl, Susan," she said. " I think you'd better leave her with her feet up——"

" Oh gosh, no," said Susan, " that would be an awful pity. If she really can walk quite well, as Fräulein Amacher says——"

"Walking's all right, I suppose," said Midge, "but lying there at your ease, with everybody running round bringing you things, what bliss!"

"Midge!" said Susan, scandalised. "That's not the way to talk!"

"I could see myself enjoying that life thoroughly," said Midge, "and I expect she does too. Why should you butt in and push the poor girl on to her feet and spoil it for her?"

Susan said solemnly, "It's very wrong to talk like that, Midge. One day you may find that you *can't* walk and how would you like that?"

"I'd love it," said Midge. "That's what I keep telling you——"

Susan couldn't believe it. To lie on a sofa all day wouldn't have suited her boundless energy at all, and for Midge to talk like that was tempting Providence, not that Susan believed for one moment that she meant it. She couldn't believe that Lise could really like it either—*somehow* she must be persuaded to get on to her feet.

They called in to see Lise nearly every day after that. Unlikely as it seemed to the modest Carmichaels, Fräulein Amacher insisted that Lise enjoyed their visits and looked forward to them. They all thought that Lise was rather spoilt and sometimes very cross, but they made allowances for her, and on the whole she was gay and good fun. In spite of Midge's assertion that there was no need to be sorry for Lise, they all were—terribly sorry for her. To have been struck down in her prime (as Susan liked to call it) seemed to the others a dreadful thing, and they felt that the least they could do was to pay her a visit occasionally. "Just as long as she doesn't start throwing things at us," said Midge.

"The only one she's likely to throw things at is Susan," said Charlotte.

Susan had tried, as tactfully as she knew how, which wasn't really an object lesson in tact, to rouse Lise. She had suggested that they should take Lise out for a row on the lake. Lise declined. Her father had ordered a small cabin-cruiser, she said, when that was ready she could be carried on board and Johann the chauffeur could take her all over the lake. Susan knew that Lise's father had given her a car which she could drive in spite of her lame leg; Susan mentioned lots of places that it would be nice to visit —wouldn't Lise like to visit them? Lise said no; she had been to Berne and Interlaken and the Rhône Glacier hundreds of times. Susan said, had Lise ever been up to Wissifluh, it was beautiful up there and the cable-railway had to be seen to be believed. Lise glanced at her sharply and asked if they had been up to Wissifluh?

"Heavens yes," said Midge. "We all nearly died of fright."

This was indignantly denied by Bill, who hadn't been frightened, and by Susan, who had forgotten.

"Did you——" Lise began, then abruptly changed the subject, and asked if they had been up the Burgen-stock yet? Susan said no, they kept meaning to. Would Lise like to go with them one day? Lise said no thank you.

Susan sighed and talked in private to Bill about

schemes for knocking Lise's chair over or pushing her into the swimming-bath accidentally or for setting off rockets and fire-crackers and things under her chair so that she would be *forced* to get to her feet, but for once Bill wouldn't have anything to do with Susan's schemes. "Oh, let's leave Lise alone and just enjoy Switzerland," he said. "Our holiday is nearly half over already——"

One Sunday morning Susan didn't waken for once to a chorus of sparrows and the distant tinkle of cow-bells and the sun rosy on the mountain tops and sparkling on the lake. The mountains were shrouded in mist, the lake was cold and grey, and the rain pattered dismally on the veranda. At breakfast every-one was rather silent and Midge said suddenly, "Good-ness, this weather just fits! I wondered why there was a cloud hanging over me and I've just remembered. This is the day that the ghastly Gascoignes arrive!"

Bill pretended to be sick, Charlotte and Susan uttered loud and exaggerated groans. Aunt Lucy immediately began to look indignant. She could never understand her family's dislike of the Gascoignes, whom she considered a clever, talented, interesting and original family. So she became immediately on the defensive and said, "Now just stop all that sort of thing all of you before you begin——"

"Are the Gascoignes arriving to-day?" said Dr. Carmichael, who apart from medical matters was inclined to be a trifle vague. "Nice little woman, Mrs. Gascoigne——"

Aunt Lucy, who seemed to lose all her habitual tact in dealing with her family where the Gascoignes were concerned, was saying, "We must meet their boat——"

"Aunt Lucy!"

"Och, jings, Aunt Lucy, we'll see them soon enough——"

"Meet the boat? No fear! I'm not going to meet that Pea-green!"

"Meet the boat? Because then we might get a chance to push them in the lake, you mean?"

"Midge, that's not the way to speak!"

"What time do these plagues of Egypt arrive?"

"I don't know. We'll meet *every* boat," said Aunt Lucy, suddenly exasperated.

By lunch-time the clouds had lifted and the sun was shining. The spirits of the Carmichaels had lifted too. For one thing, it was almost impossible to be gloomy in Rosendorf, that gay and flower-decked place. On their way to meet the boat for the first time they had found a concert in progress in the Music Pavilion on the Kurplatz beside the lake and a bevy of young people in national costume gaily dancing. Susan and the Carmichaels weren't going to miss this for any silly old Gascoignes. In the afternoon they went to the bathing-beach in the funny little electric conveyance, like a toy train, that plied between the pier and the bathing-beach, and took turns in rushing back to the pier to meet boats. No Gascoignes fortunately appeared. But the Carmichaels could hardly expect this luck to continue. They all stood assembled on the pier waiting for the last boat of the day.

"I dread that Pea-green," Susan confessed. "I expect

his imagination will be allowed free rein as usual and he'll be pretending to be wild animals and things all over Switzerland and jumping on me——"

"P'raps he'll have a new line," Midge said.

He had. It didn't turn out to be an improvement. The boat came in. They saw Gabrielle and Mrs. Gascoigne at once, both dressed alike in tight black jeans, laced with pink, and pink blouses. Behind them was Adrian wearing, of all things, a bowler hat.

"Oh *help*," said Midge. "Do we have to walk through the village with them got up like that?"

The boat tied up beside the pier. Mrs. Gascoigne and Gabrielle waved happily and began to shout greetings and remarks in loud voices which made Susan and the Carmichaels feel acutely embarrassed. Adrian solemnly raised his bowler hat. Suddenly Susan felt something hard sticking into her ribs. She glanced down and saw that it was a gun, with Peregrine at the other end of it.

"Stick 'em up!" said Peregrine. "Reach for the sky!"

Susan yelled and clutched Midge round the neck. "Don't be dotty, Susie," said Midge, unclutching Susan's arms. "It's not loaded."

"That's what you think," said Peregrine.

Susan could hear Gabrielle and Mrs. Gascoigne trilling with merry laughter as they came across the gangway.

"Peregrine, you really are the naughtiest boy I know," said Mrs. Gascoigne fondly. "Now you mustn't frighten Susan any more——" She turned to Susan and whispered in a confidential aside, "My dear," she said, "you needn't worry, he *always* misses——"

"If ever I get my hands on that gun *I'll* not miss," murmured Midge.

The last they saw of Peregrine that night he was riding in the luggage cart behind the porter's bicycle on top of the luggage, happily taking pot-shots at the passers-by with his pellet-gun.

CHAPTER EIGHT

HAPPY DAYS WITH THE GASCOIGNES

THEY SAW him the first thing in the morning. The Carmichaels and Susan were peacefully having breakfast next morning when suddenly the muzzle of a gun appeared among the nasturtiums. "Stick 'em up!" said Peregrine through his teeth.

Susan gave a yelp and jumped about two inches off her chair.

"Good morning, Peregrine," said Aunt Lucy mildly. "You oughtn't to point your gun at people even if it isn't loaded——"

"It is loaded," said Peregrine. "And how can I shoot a person if I don't point the gun at her?"

"Who are you planning to shoot?" asked Susan with a ghastly attempt at friendliness.

"You," said Peregrine.

He stretched a hand above the nasturtiums, snatched a roll, all deliciously buttered and spread with honey, off Susan's plate and disappeared.

"Sweet little chap, isn't he?" said Charlotte.

Aunt Lucy looked slightly abashed.

Their next visitor was Adrian. He appeared at the window looking handsome in very short shorts and a garish American shirt. He bade them good-morning, absent-mindedly helping himself to a roll, all deliciously buttered and spread with honey, off Susan's plate, and told them that his mamma and Gabrielle were still resting.

"Well, that's something," muttered Susan. "That gives me an equal chance of being allowed to eat my last roll." She hunched herself protectively round her plate and resolved that as far as she was concerned *anybody* could have the hitherto coveted seat at the window while the Gascoignes were still in Rosendorf.

"We thought it might be fun to go up Mount Pilatus to-day," Adrian went on. "You *will* all come, won't you?"

"As if he owned Pilatus," said Midge furiously as they were gathering up cardigans, cameras, lunches and the usual paraphernalia for the expedition. "I knew these ghastly Gascoignes would ruin our holiday."

Susan said that even the Gascoignes couldn't ruin Switzerland.

They did their best, in Midge's opinion. To begin with, those awful clothes! This morning Mrs. Gascoigne and Gabrielle arrived at the pier an hour late in very tight tartan jeans and yellow blouses which matched Peregrine's shirt. Bill refused to be seen with them. He slunk away to a remote and not very comfortable corner of the boat hoping he would be safe there. Adrian talked to Charlotte, and Midge and Susan were left with Gabrielle who patronised them as usual and told them that it was such a pity that they didn't know the language. Selina (as she always called her mother) had always had foreign governesses for her and Adrian and Peregrine and they could speak German and French and Italian and even

Swiss almost as well as English. It must be frightfully dull, she said, not knowing what everybody was saying.

Pity Selina didn't teach you how to behave, instead of all those languages, Susan thought, but she said nothing, only tried not to listen to Gabrielle but to concentrate on the beauties of the morning, the lake as smooth as silk and Pilatus slightly misty with heat in the distance; and watched Peregrine, who of course had brought his gun with him, out of the tail of her eye. They changed boats at a nice little place called Kehrsiten where there was a shop as usual, everything laid out enticingly, where Bill bought a *stocknagel*, one of the little tin medallions that people nailed to their sticks to show to what places and mountains they had been; and Gabrielle and Adrian disgraced the Carmichaels by putting a franc in the juke-box (the only one they ever came across in Switzerland) and jiving to the American jazz that blared out while the quiet Swiss people looked on in amazement. Susan and the Carmichaels were thankful when their next boat arrived. This took them to a village called Alpnachstadt where a little red funicular was waiting for them. It was built in steps, and the railway seemed to Susan to go straight up in the air, but the guard had securely fastened them in and the dizzy heights had no terrors for her when she was safely in the train. The lake spread out below them; beside the railway line were the wonderful mountain flowers, and the alpenrose, with its pink flowers and leaves of rusty green, grew everywhere over the grey rocks. Susan's ears began to crack and ache, but so apparently did Peregrine's, which was some comfort—she hoped *she* didn't get into such a state as he did—he doubled himself up, holding his ears and rocking from side to side while Selina fussed over him and Aunt Lucy gave him barley sugar.

There was more than one peak, they found, at the top, with a hotel perched on the saddle between. A narrow path, with dizzy vistas stretching hundreds of feet below, wound up to the summit. Bill kept between Susan and the sheer drops, for it was useless for her to pretend any longer that she liked heights. Peregrine said, "Are you frightened, Susan, shall I take your hand?" but Bill gave him a good clout for such cheek when his mother wasn't looking and Susan had no further trouble with him on that score. At the top a stout wall had been provided, which was a great relief, and she was able to walk about quite boldly and look over the wall and gaze at a smudge on the far-distant horizon which somebody said was the Black Forest. Huge black birds with gleaming feathers, red feet and yellow bills hopped tamely about their legs, looking for titbits from picnickers. Susan wondered if they were ravens, but not even the Gascoignes, who usually knew everything, could tell her.

They had lunch on the terrace of the hotel and the birds came and perched on the rail and ate from their hands. Far away they could see the mountains of the Bernese Alps, the Eiger, the Mönch and the Jungfrau and near at hand an occasional solitary figure, with stick and rucksack, walked down the path or from the other peaks, across the grim, bare, stony slope. Nobody, Midge noted thankfully, suggested that they should walk down this mountain.

After lunch, Susan and Bill and Midge decided to explore a little, and Peregrine and Gabrielle finished off the Carmichaels' food. "In spite of all the remarks about how beautifully packed their lunch is, and how dainty," Bill muttered to Susan, "it seems to me they're mighty anxious to get their hands on ours!"

Peregrine disappeared and the others visited the usual little shop which even managed to flourish on top of Mount Pilatus, and wandered down the slope, under the terrace of the hotel. Suddenly something went *ping* past Susan's ear. She spun round and caught sight of Peregrine darting out of sight behind a rock. She bounded up the slope and was on him. Stuttering with rage and fright she had just grabbed the gun from him, when another figure appeared round a bend in the path with a roar of rage. He planted himself in front of Susan and shook his fist in her face. Clutching the gun she backed a couple of steps, looking bewildered. Then he tore off his hat and pointed a finger trembling with rage at it. Susan politely peered at the hat and at a neat little hole drilled through the felt of the crown. She smiled uncertainly. " 'Mm. Very nice," she said, not knowing at all what she was expected to say.

"Nice?" shrieked the man. "It ees not nice! To be shot at, to be very almost killed, ees that nice?"

Susan said no, it wasn't. She had just been shot at herself, she went on chattily, and it wasn't a bit nice——

"Then why you shoot at me?" shouted the man. "Assassin!"

Susan was quite bewildered. "Me? Shoot at you?"

she gasped. Honestly, she was thinking nervously, he can't be right in the head, when suddenly she realised that she was holding the gun. "Oh *gosh*," she said, "did you think—oh *help*—oh I say, I'm terribly sorry but truly——"

"Sorry? *Bah!*" shouted the furious man. He jammed his wounded hat back on his head and strode off.

Midge and Gabrielle and Bill came from behind a boulder, laughing.

"Jings, it's not funny!" cried Susan. "He thought I shot him!"

"I know!" gasped Midge between puffs of laughter. "And I dare say it's not funny, but your face——!"

"Where's that Pea-green?" muttered Susan. "I'll riddle him so full of holes he'll look like a colander——"

Peregrine of course had vanished. He appeared a minute or two later with Aunt Lucy and Mrs. Gascoigne. "Selina," he said in his high pedantic voice, "I don't think I ought to let Susan have my gun, do you? She might shoot somebody. Or even shoot one of those heavenly, beautiful birds——"

Aunt Lucy gasped, and taking the pellet-gun firmly from Susan's nerveless grasp she handed it to Mrs. Gascoigne.

"Oh, Peregrine, *darling*, *do* take this dreadful lethal weapon from me," said Selina, laughing gaily. "Or it will be the death of me!"

"Death of her!" muttered Susan under her breath to Midge. "I wish it *could* be the death of her! And the death of Pea-green *and* Adrian *and* that stuck-up Gabrielle!"

"Susie," said Midge, "calm yourself. The only person it's at all likely to be the death of is you——"

Susan said that she wouldn't be surprised. She was still brooding on the unfairness of life when they gathered at the steep stone steps of the terminus and piled into the little train. To her horror she nearly got in with the man whom Peregrine had shot—she backed out of that compartment, which was a nuisance for the people behind on whom she trampled, with great speed, but not before she noticed that beside the shot man was someone whose face was familiar and would be familiar, she thought, until her dying day—the man who had nearly pushed her under the car in the Kapellgasse ! Later she told Midge and Charlotte and Bill, but all *they* said was that her troubles with Pea-green were turning her brain.

And then there was the day they sailed up the lake, Peregrine just about spoilt that day. They sailed to Brunnen and had lunch there, and then round to the furthermost point of the lake, to Flüelen; and on the way they saw William Tell's chapel and a memorial to a man called Schiller who was a poet, Uncle Charles told them, who wrote a play about William Tell. They stopped at a tiny little quaintly-carved pier called Rütli and Uncle Charles told them that in a meadow nearby the Swiss republic had been born, for there three Swiss patriots had met secretly and vowed to rebel against the hated tyranny of Austria. They were all very much interested in this story, except apparently Peregrine—for he wandered off, in which direction it was all too apparent when the boat left the pier and they saw Peregrine come rushing on to the pier shouting and waving his arms; and, when the boat didn't immediately turn back for him, dancing up and down and stamping with rage.

"Heavens, what a relief," said Midge, "we'll have peace for the rest of the trip——"

But of course Midge was reckoning without the other Gascoignes. Mrs. Gascoigne went on as if Peregrine had been marooned on a desert island, and Gabrielle went on about poor little Peregrine, how lonely and frightened he would be, and Adrian went on about how his mamma was not to worry, that he would go right back on the next boat to Rütli and find poor little Peregrine——

"You can't," said Bill, studying his time-table, "unless you want to stay at Rütli all night."

"Such a fuss," Midge said to Susan, and Susan, who really didn't much care how lonely and frightened Pea-green might be—he had frightened her often enough, after all—yet who couldn't help interfering, said why didn't *all* the Gascoignes get off at the next village, which was Treib, and wait there for Pea-green, sorry, Peregrine?

"And break up the party!" cried Mrs. Gascoigne. "Oh, we couldn't do that!"

"We'll all get off at Treib and wait for poor little Peregrine," said Aunt Lucy, carefully avoiding the eyes of her furious nieces and nephew.

At Treib there was a heavenly old house, dated 1639, most beautifully carved and decorated and ornamented with window-boxes full of petunias. It was built over the lake and nice little boats were moored under it. But after everybody had admired it and taken photographs of it there wasn't a great deal to do. Uncle Charles suggested looking for a hotel or a café where they could get cold drinks, but Mrs. Gascoigne said that she simply daren't leave the pier in case she somehow missed her poor darling. She hated being a nuisance and they must all just go off and leave her, but she *must* be on the pier when the next boat arrived. So everybody sat around for an hour, and Susan and Midge invented all manner of tortures for poor darling Peregrine in low voices until Gabrielle spoilt such innocent pleasures by suggesting that they should all play a guessing game to pass the time, which everybody hated and was very bad at, except the Gascoignes.

The next boat arrived, but there was no sign of Peregrine. Now Mrs. Gascoigne was in a fix—should they assume that Peregrine was on the boat some-where and get on themselves, or assume that he *wasn't* and wait for the next one? The Carmichaels said that he was sure to be on it—no doubt he was below, or on the starboard side, hidden from them. The Gascoignes said never—of *course* he would expect them to be waiting for him at the next stop, and if he was on the boat he would be hanging over the side looking out for them. As they argued, a few passengers got off and a few passengers got on and the boat sailed away. It didn't improve the tempers of the Carmichaels when Susan pointed out a small figure, leaning over the stern and talking animatedly and showing off his gun to someone by his side.

The Carmichaels were furious; Susan, however, had completely lost interest in the nuisance value of Peregrine. She drew Midge and Bill on one side, in a dither of excitement. "Did you see who Peregrine was talking to?" she asked.

Midge said that the red mist of rage in front of her eyes had prevented her seeing anything.

"Well it was that man who pushed me under the car in the Kapellgasse!" said Susan. "He's following us! This is the second time that I've seen him, third if you count the Kapellgasse! We saw him up Mount Pilatus and now again to-day! He's following us and it all must have something to do with the tea! There *is* some mystery about Fräulein Amacher and her pound of tea!"

"Nonsense," said Midge. "The only mystery is how Pea-green could have lived so long without somebody murdering him."

Peregrine was in a rage when, at last, on the last boat, tired, hungry and late for dinner, they reached Rosendorf. "I've been waiting here *hours* for you," he said severely.

"*You've* been waiting for *us*, you little——" began Susan.

"Oh, climb up a tree and branch off," said Peregrine.

Then there was the perfectly ghastly evening they spent with the Gascoignes at their hotel.

"To-night there is to be yodelling and then dancing at our hotel," said Gabrielle as they lay on the grass in the garden of the Chalet du Lac sun-bathing after their swim one morning. "Selina said would you like to come or are you too young to go out after dinner?"

"Of course we're not too young!" Susan said indignantly. "We're the same age as you are!"

"We thought it would be a change for you as I don't suppose your little hotel has anything like that," Gabrielle went on, ignoring Susan.

"As a matter of fact there's a concert followed by dancing in our hotel every Monday," said Susan. "The Rosendorf orchestra goes round the hotels—the *principal* hotels—in turn. Haven't they been to your hotel?"

"Heavens, this isn't that footling little orchestra," said Gabrielle, "this is a proper company of Swiss yodellers. I've heard of them as a matter of fact, they're excellent. You won't forget to dress, will you, our hotel is rather fussy about that——?"

After Gabrielle had left them Susan burst out indignantly, "Jings, *she's* one to talk about dressing! A pair of jeans and a grubby blouse is all you ever see her in! And she has the cheek to tell *us* what to wear!"

However, as she might have known, the Gascoignes succeeded in making them feel uncomfortable as usual, for when Uncle Charles and Aunt Lucy and Bill arrived, accompanied by the girls wearing fresh crisp cotton dresses in which they all looked very nice indeed, they found Adrian in a dinner jacket, Mrs. Gascoigne in a ballerina-length gown that shimmered, and Gabrielle in a long nylon party frock and wearing lipstick. In the Carmichael family only Charlotte was allowed to wear lipstick.

"Oh, you haven't changed after all?" murmured Gabrielle as she came to meet them.

"We have changed," said Susan through her teeth. "These are our best dresses——"

"Really? Oh well—well, come and sit down, we have a table near the band——"

The garden of the Hotel Splendide was looking very gay and festive. Fairy lights were threaded through the trees under which people were sitting at little tables. Beyond the low wall the lake lapped gently, silvered by the rising moon. Round the curve of the bay the lights of Rosendorf danced in the water. Pale swans glided up to the wall and glided away again, leaving scarcely a ripple on the stillness of the lake. Over by the terrace of the hotel was a place for dancing and a platform for the yodellers.

"Nobody's wearing grand clothes like the ghastly Gascoignes," Susan managed to whisper to Midge. "Adrian's is the only dinner jacket. It's just as bad to be too grand as to be not grand enough, isn't it?"

"Worse," Midge murmured. "I'd say we were just right, but they always make you feel you've put on the wrong clothes. And have you noticed how greedy the people are in this hotel? All simply stuffing themselves with cakes——"

Mrs. Gascoigne was arranging her guests in her most charming way (although as Bill pointed out later they weren't really her guests since Uncle Charles paid for everybody, and anybody in Rosendorf could come to this concert if they wanted to, you didn't have to be staying at the Splendide). Then the yodellers arrived and Susan and her cousins stopped being cross with the ghastly Gascoignes and gave themselves up to enjoyment. The yodellers wore their national costume—white shirts, short black velvet jackets with bright buttons and gold and orange trimming; they wore little round caps and some had edelweiss embroidered on their lapels.

Mrs. Gascoigne and Uncle Charles were ordering coffee with cream for the grown-ups and lemonade for the young people. Peregrine was ordering cakes and ice-creams.

"Where d'you put it, Peregrine?" Aunt Lucy said, laughing. "It takes me all my time to swallow a few sips of coffee after these enormous Swiss dinners——"

"Oh my dear, we can't resist them!" said Mrs. Gascoigne. "We're all going to have cakes, aren't we, darlings ? There's a coffee-meringue that's out of this world and a sort of praline—we all drool at the mouth!"

The choir sang three yodelling songs and then had a rest while everybody danced. One of the yodellers asked Mrs. Gascoigne to dance, first asking Adrian very politely if he might dance with his sister. "Isn't it too sweet?" Mrs. Gascoigne whispered. "They always think I'm Adrian's sister!" She whirled off in a very lively old-fashioned waltz.

"You look much nicer than anybody's old sister," Bill muttered fiercely to Aunt Lucy, who laughed and danced with Uncle Charles. A nice young round-faced yodeller asked Charlotte to dance; Adrian danced with Midge. Bill thought to himself how uncomfortable the Gascoignes were—their clothes always different from everybody else's and always making you feel wrong. As Bill was wearing his first pair of long trousers he didn't, as a matter of fact, feel wrong, he felt wonderful; but growing so elderly had its disadvantages too, for he supposed, he thought, sighing sadly, he'd have to live up to his trousers and ask Gabrielle to dance—it was just as well that Aunt Lucy had forced him to go to that frightful dancing class. He and Gabrielle got up.

"Come on, Susan, I suppose I'll have to dance with you seeing you're a wallflower," said Peregrine.

"There's not the least need," said Susan stiffly, "unless you want to dance. Are you sure you *can* dance?"

"Of course——"

She found his method of dancing was to whirl her round and round extremely fast, bumping into as many people as possible and blaming Susan. When the music stopped Susan was so dizzy that she could hardly stand. "Pea-green," she muttered, "*help* me! My head's going round like a peerie, if you know what that means——"

"Of course I don't know what your rough Scotch words mean," said Peregrine.

"Well, it means a top, and my head's going round like one. Help me!" She grabbed at Peregrine's shoulder, but as he happened to slip out of her grasp at that point she found herself grabbing at a total stranger instead, a large fat jolly-looking Swiss gentleman. As he wasn't really expecting the full weight of Susan to be launched against him, he lurched forward, knocked into his partner, who in turn cannoned into a table and unfortunately tipped a bottle of wine over a lady and gentleman who were sitting there. Everybody milled round in great confusion, exclaiming and apologising and mopping up the mess, except Susan who, nearly dead with embarrassment, stood with her eyes shut clutching a chair, while her head whirled round and she wished the Hotel Splendide would fall on top of her and bury her, or the lake rise up and drown her, and vowing that one day, *one day*, she really would murder Pea-green. When the whirling in her head had steadied a little she murmured excuse me, please, in a very shame-faced way and crept back to their table where she found Peregrine explaining in his high voice that some people would never make good dancers because they were so clumsy and had such big feet.

But the embarrassments of the evening were not yet over. After the next group of yodelling songs Peregrine left their table and went and spoke to the leader of the band; and the next thing that Susan and the Carmichaels knew, Peregrine was standing up on the front of the platform reciting! As bold as brass, standing there reciting in German! And the strange thing was, everybody seemed to be enjoying it! Not only the ghastly Gascoignes, who were nearly doubled up with laughter, but lots of other people were laughing like anything too. Even Aunt Lucy and Uncle Charles laughed a little, although Susan was jolly sure that *they* didn't know what they were laughing at. Only Susan and her cousins didn't laugh. They sat with straight faces, wishing that either they, or preferably Pea-green, would drop dead. When the dreadful boy had finished, he bowed and started off on another piece of great length, a serious, dramatic one this time. After what seemed like hours to the shamed Carmichaels, he bowed again and came back to their table. Susan was horrified to notice that people were staring not only at Peregrine but at all of them. She lowered her eyes and blushed. Mrs. Gascoigne leant over and kissed Peregrine. "Darling!" she said. "*So* good! *E*verybody loved it!"

Midge leant over to Susan and whispered, "Darling! *So* good! I'm going to be sick!"

"Let's go," Susan muttered back. They unobtrusively slipped away and sat on the wall among the shadows, gazing gloomily at the lights of Rosendorf reflected in the water and the lights of their own nice peaceful Chalet du Lac twinkling softly in the distance.

"I couldn't listen to that Selina drooling over Peagreen another minute," Susan said. "What was he reciting *for*? Who asked him to get up and recite?"

"D'you think they'd like a turn from me?" Midge murmured. "Song and dance? Or a tune on my recorder?"

Susan giggled and felt better. "Isn't he a beastly little show-off?" she said. "One good thing, everybody was hating it——"

"I wish I could be sure of that," said Midge. "It seemed to me that they were all enjoying his recitations thoroughly——"

"Let's stay here and enjoy the yodellers in peace," Susan suggested. "The ghastly Gascoignes spoil everything——"

The wall was hard, and became rather cold and certainly uncomfortable, but it was better than being with the Gascoignes. A swan came up inquiringly. "Och," said Susan, "I wish I had some crusts for him——" She glanced towards their table and saw that no one was sitting there. "I'll slip over and grab one of those sandwiches the Ghastlys ordered—jings, aren't they greedy? They've been guzzling cakes and sandwiches all evening——"

She went to their table and picked up a sandwich from the plate; and as she did so she glanced at the dancers to see if any of the Gascoignes had their eyes on her. Adrian and Gabrielle, her horse's tail flying, were jiving in a corner, Peregrine was being unobtrusively kept under control by Aunt Lucy, Uncle Charles was thumping gravely round with Charlotte, Selina—Susan caught her breath—Selina was dancing with the man from the Kapellgasse!

Susan could hardly believe her eyes. Again that man had turned up! She stood staring at the dancers, her mouth open. The music stopped, the couples were leaving the floor. Susan suddenly came to life again, grabbed the sandwich and slipped away through the trees. "Ducky, the swan has gone *ages* ago," Midge murmured. "I told him to wait, but he said he couldn't hang about here all night——"

Susan collapsed weakly on the wall and gripped Midge's arm. "Midge!" she said, round-eyed, "that man is *here*!"

Midge gently released her arm. "What man?" she said.

"The man from the Kapellgasse! The man who

tried to push me under a car! He was dancing with Selina!"

"D'you think there's any chance of him pushing Selina under a car?" Midge said hopefully.

"Och, do be *serious*——" Susan said urgently.

"Oh here you are," said Gabrielle, coming up to them in a flurry of nylon and stiffened petticoats. "Why are you lurking in this dark corner? No partners?"

Susan put her hand behind her back and dropped the sandwich into the water. "We're having a rest," she said. "We find little boys like Pea-green, sorry, Peregrine, very tiring."

"I suppose a gifted little boy like Peregrine does take more living up to than the dull-witted kind like Bill," Gabrielle said sweetly.

Susan felt the blood rushing to her head, but before she could spring to the defence of Bill, Midge changed the subject. "Who was Selina dancing with just now?" she asked in her calm, lazy voice.

"She has danced with so many——" Gabrielle began.

Susan, forcing herself to keep her temper, said, "This last time—a young man with flaxen hair——"

"Oh that's Herr Gruber," said Gabrielle, "he's staying here——"

"Staying *here*?"

"Yes. He's somebody quite famous but I can't remember what. He's a *great* friend of ours——"

Bill came over. "We're going home now," he said. "Aunt Lucy sent me to find you——"

Susan and Midge got up. Susan was pleased to

notice out of the corner of her eye that a swan was polishing off the remains of a wet and soggy sandwich. At least the poor old swan had got something out of the evening, Susan thought. All she had got, she felt, was a lot of worry. That man *here*! Right here in Rosendorf! What *did* it all mean?

CHAPTER NINE

SUSAN TRIES TO HELP

SUSAN COULDN'T get over the fact of the man in the Kapellgasse being actually there in Rosendorf!

"Now will you believe me?" she asked the others as they were sitting in the garden after breakfast the next morning. "Every movement we make is being watched!"

"If you ask *me*," said Midge, "it's every movement that the Gascoignes make that's being watched. After all, it's their hotel in which he has installed himself!"

"If you ask *me*," said Charlotte, "Susie is off her nut. Oh, I admit that we've seen this man two or three times and I admit that he's the same man whom we saw in the Kapellgasse. What I *don't* admit is that he tried to push Susie under a car—much as he might have wanted to——"

Charlotte was rather cross this morning. Her evening at the Hotel Splendide hadn't been a complete success either. Adrian, who had been in the habit of showing her quite a lot of attention had apparently switched his attentions to Lise. The Carmichaels, who naturally hadn't neglected Lise when the Gascoignes had arrived, had been obliged rather reluctantly to introduce them to each other. Of course the Gascoignes had all made a tremendous fuss of Lise—in fact you would think, Midge remarked once, that

Lise was the Gascoignes' discovery—and last night at the hotel, although Adrian had danced with Charlotte quite a lot he had talked about Lise all the time—how beautiful she was! How tragic her story! How rich her father, Charlotte added to herself rather sourly. Of course she didn't care *who* Adrian talked about—she wasn't in the least interested, far less jealous, she wasn't even sure if she *liked* Adrian, only he was at least the best of the Gascoignes—not that she could stand any of them and she wished that Susan and Midge and Bill wouldn't talk about them all day long. "—And do stop nattering on about those Gascoignes," she finished up, and then gave her attention to the little oil that she was painting of Pilatus from the garden of the Chalet du Lac.

Midge looked at Susan with raised eyebrows. What was the matter with Charlotte? They had been talking about that man in the Kapellgasse Gruber or whatever his name was, and not about the Gascoignes at all—Not that *she* wanted to talk about the Gascoignes or ever see them again if that were possible—— "Let's go along to see Lise," she said, "and with any luck we'll miss the Ghastlys. Coming, Charlotte?"

"I'm busy," Charlotte said shortly.

"Okay," said Midge peaceably. "You stay here, and if the Ghastlys come you don't know where we are——"

Lise wasn't in very good form either when they arrived. She seemed to be rather depressed, and said that she was tired of Rosendorf—she thought that it would be a good idea to go back to Zürich where her home was, the See Perle being only a summer chalet.

Or it might be fun to make her father and Fräulein Amacher take her on a tour of Italy or Greece or some place more interesting than boring Lake Lucerne. Only she couldn't imagine anything more boring than sitting in a car all day. Susan and Midge and Bill listened without comment—*they* couldn't understand how anyone could ever find Lake Lucerne boring. " I suppose you all went to the Splendide last night to hear the yodellers," Lise went on. " Adrian asked me to go but of course I couldn't——"

Oh ho, thought Midge, was that why Charlotte was so cross?

Susan said, " You should have gone, Lise, it was fun——"

" Fun for you, perhaps," said Lise, " but for me? Not much fun for me to sit watching everybody dance——"

" Help," said Midge, " dancing with the Gascoignes wasn't much fun I can tell you! In fact Pea-green was an absolute menace, wasn't he, Susan? "

But Susan wasn't listening to Midge. She had knelt up straight on the grass looking alert, for all the world, said Bill afterwards, like a terrier getting the first faint whiff of a rat. Was this her chance? Susan thought. " But Lise," she said, " you could have danced too——"

Lise glared at her.

" Why *don't* you try? " said Susan eagerly. " At least, dancing may be a bit difficult for you, but you could walk! Fräulein Amacher says you can walk, why don't you walk? "

" Because I waddle like a duck! " Lise said savagely.

"Oh," said Susan, a little damped. "But Lise," she went on, ignoring Lise's tight lips and furious eyes, "supposing you do waddle like a duck? It doesn't much matter *how* you walk really as long as you can get about——"

"It matters to me!" cried Lise. "I was pretty before this beastly thing happened to me! I was the prettiest of all my friends, the most graceful, the best dancer! Why should this happen to *me*?"

"Why shouldn't it happen to you?" cried Susan indignantly. "Polio can happen to anybody. You're not somebody special, you're not made of different stuff from other people. It would have been just as bad for any other girl—her life would have been just as much spoilt as yours—it would have been awful for anybody. But what makes *me* cross is that your life *isn't* spoilt, you don't *have* to lie here, a helpless cripple—lots of people are crippled after polio and *can't* walk—but you could walk if you liked, only you won't try just because you're too conceited or something——!"

Midge and Bill were fidgeting uncomfortably. Lise was looking at Susan as if she couldn't believe her ears: she was very pale and her hands gripped the sides of her chair. When Susan paused for breath she almost screamed with rage. "Be quiet! How *dare* you speak to me like that " Her English deserted her and she spoke furiously in Swiss. Then she picked up a book from the table beside her chair and threw it at Susan with all her force. "Get out! *Get out! GET OUT!*" she cried and burst into tears.

Midge and Bill, horribly embarrassed, glanced at

Susan, who was still sitting on the grass, looking down at the piece of paper which had fluttered out of the book. They rose, but Susan didn't move. "Susan," said Midge, "didn't you hear Lise? She told you to get out . . . *Susan!*"

Susan looked up vacantly. "What?" she said.

"Come on," said Bill through his teeth. He and Midge moved off across the grass.

"Oh!" said Susan. "Oh, of course——" She scrambled to her feet.

But in the midst of her tears Lise suddenly began to laugh—a watery uncertain laugh. "Oh," she cried in exasperation, "how can one be angry with such a girl! Come back!" she called.

"No fear," muttered Midge. "She might hit *me* next time!"

"Please come back!" Lise called.

Midge and Bill and Susan walked slowly back across the grass. Lise had stopped crying and had scrubbed her eyes with a handkerchief. She looked as pretty as ever—prettier if anything, her gentian-blue eyes drowned in tears. "Don't go," she said. "It looks so silly to go off like that, one, two, three in a row. Besides Fräulein Amacher would be angry with me— although it is you she should be angry with, you interfering girl," she added in a waspish aside to Susan. "Sit down and I will say I am sorry. I will not mean it, but I will say it——"

Midge said coldly, "Don't bother to say sorry if you don't mean it. But you shouldn't, as a matter of fact, take Susan too seriously either. She doesn't mean to be interfering, she just can't stop herself trying to help——"

Susan, who seemed to have come out of her trance, and who felt simply *awful*, thought that it was jolly loyal of Midge to talk like that considering the ghastly mess she had just made of everything. "Of *course* I didn't mean to interfere, Lise, honestly I didn't," she said earnestly, "it was only that you seemed to be missing such a lot lying here all day when there was no *need*——"

"*I* know what I am missing," said Lise.

Midge said, "Oh help, *Susan*, don't start all over again," and Susan said that she wouldn't.

Susan and Midge and Bill left soon after that, on quite amiable terms again with Lise. As they walked back to the Chalet du Lac Midge said, "Perhaps that very disagreeable scene will encourage you to stop interfering——"

"What?" said Susan vacantly.

"Oh gosh," said Bill, "she's gone into a trance again."

"Oh, Susie, do *listen*! What is the matter with you? You cause a scene like that and then you don't even know what I'm talking about!"

"I can't make it out at all!" said Susan.

"*Susan!*" said Midge very slowly and firmly. "I'm talking to you! Please listen! If you don't stop poking your nose into other people's business and causing scenes——"

"Oh I know, wasn't it *ghastly*?" said Susan easily. "I felt such a fool. But of course if she hadn't thrown the book at me I shouldn't have seen the cutting——"

Midge and Bill stared at her. At last Midge said reluctantly, "What cutting?"

"Well, didn't you see it fall out of the book?" Susan asked. "It came out of the book and landed right at my knee. My eyes nearly dropped out of my head because it was about that boy up at Wissifluh." Midge and Bill gazed at her, bereft of speech. Susan was beaming delightedly. "Yes, great big headlines— FAMOUS SCIENTIST'S SON DISAPPEARS FROM PRAGUE—in English you know, on that terribly thin paper——"

"An airmail edition of an English newspaper, you mean?" asked Bill.

"Yes—you know—Uncle Charles gets one sometimes. He said it was a special edition flown over from London——"

"But what's all this got to do with the boy at Wissifluh?" said Midge weakly.

"Well, he's Rudi Pancake, isn't he? Well, this piece in the paper was all about him! He's the son of a famous scientist who escaped from Prague or some place like that behind the Iron Curtain, and now his son has disappeared too! At least the paper said that the authorities denied it, but that the boy's friends say he has gone! And there he is up at Wissifluh! Isn't it exciting!"

Bill said *gosh*, it certainly *was* and even Midge said that it was jolly extraordinary. Susan's eyes were sparkling. "This boy, Rudi Pancake, has been smuggled out of Prague," she said, "jings, I wonder if Fräulein Amacher did it!" Midge and Bill shrieked with laughter at the idea of elderly, respectable Fräulein

Amacher smuggling boys from behind the Iron Curtain. "Well, she had something to do with it!" said Susan imperturbably. "I told you she was smuggling people, didn't I? I expect she'll smuggle him off somewhere else as soon as the excitement has died down! That was his passport we brought in the pound of tea—no wonder it had to be smuggled in! I bet there are spies everywhere—that ghastly Frau Tannenbaum! And Herr Bruger—he's certainly a spy and I understand the whole thing now!"

"It's more than I do," said Midge.

"Well, it's easy—Frau Tannenbaum knew that there was something important in the parcel and tried to get it from us. She pretended that Fräulein Amacher had gone away so that we'd hand it over to her! Jings, I'm glad we didn't! And when we wouldn't hand it over, she sent Herr Gruber to push me under a car and grab it!"

Midge said that it all seemed very peculiar to her. And a pity too, she thought, there would be no holding Susan now that her view that there was something queer about the boy at Wissifluh seemed to be justified. "Just as long as you don't go interfering, Susan," she said. "It's none of your business, don't forget——"

"Couldn't we just take a wee trip up to Wissifluh?" said Susan wistfully.

"Never!" said Midge explosively. "You'll never find me in that contraption again!"

Susan pictured it and was inclined to agree with her.

"Besides," Bill said, "if Herr Bruger is a spy as you

say, why d'you imagine he is still hanging round us?"

"I can't imagine," said Susan. "It seems a waste of time to me——"

"Don't kid yourself," said Bill, "he's not wasting his time. My guess is that on account of us having had the parcel he thinks we're in the plot and that we know about the boy and he's hoping that we'll lead him to wherever the boy is! How's that for a theory?"

"Rotten," said Midge. "It's the Gascoignes whom he's hanging round, not us. Gabrielle is probably right and he has taken a fancy to Selina."

"Nonsense," said Susan, who couldn't believe that anyone could take a fancy to Selina. "That's a blind. He has the sense to know that *we* wouldn't let him hang around after what he did in the Kapellgasse so he hangs around them as the next best thing. Probably thinks they are friends of ours. Probably pumps Pea-green all the time—What are your friends doing to-day, little boy?—that sort of thing."

"It all seems a bit far-fetched to me," said Midge. "But in any case we had better not go near Wissifluh."

"No, better not," said Susan, with a small sigh. "And," she went on, cheering up, "Lise obviously knows all about it, perhaps she'll tell us the whole story one day——"

"She never will," Midge said cunningly, "if you behave like you did this morning."

"Oh help, *no*," said Susan. "I made a ghastly mess of that, didn't I?"

"So," said Midge, "don't you think that really and

truly it's time you learned to mind your own business? And leave Lise alone?"

"Och *yes*," said Susan. "I'll never *breathe* another word to Lise. And Midge, I really will try to mind my own business, I really will try——"

In about ten minutes she was plunged into another affair that couldn't possibly be described as her business. Gabrielle was at the Chalet du Lac when they got back. She had come along to ask Dr. Carmichael to go and have a look at Peregrine, who was having one of his periodic bouts of what Selina called an upset tummy, brought on by being so sensitive and highly-strung, and what Dr. Carmichael called colly-wobbles, brought on by over-eating. All those cakes and ices he ate last night, said Susan to herself when she heard. Serve the little perisher right.

Midge said cautiously that she didn't suppose that the Gascoignes would be going up a mountain or anything to-day as they wouldn't want to leave Pea-green, sorry, Peregrine.

"Oh, we weren't going very far to-day anyway," said Gabrielle. "We're expecting a great friend of ours to arrive——"

Susan had forgotten that practically everybody you'd ever heard of was a great friend of the Gascoignes —they knew writers, actors, artists, television stars, people in the B.B.C., publishers, professors, archæologists. They may have known some ordinary grocers and bank-clerks and schoolmasters as well, but if so they didn't mention them. She might have known, Susan thought, that some of their friends would be sure to turn up in Switzerland. Midge and Charlotte (who was still rather gloomily crouched over her painting) kept resolutely silent, but Susan could not resist saying, "Oh, who?"

"Gina Prescott her name is, I don't suppose you've heard of her but she's a frightfully well-known person. She's on that travel magazine called *Going Places* and she's coming to Rosendorf to see if the hotels are any good. If they are she mentions them in her articles. She's staying at our hotel, of course—"

Long after Gabrielle had gone Susan was still droning on about Miss Prescott. "Why should she go to the Gascoignes' hotel? Ours is far nicer and it would help Herr and Frau Stocker if their hotel got a boost. How do the Gascoignes know all these people? I think it's jolly mean taking her to their hotel—the others should have a chance too. I wish I could work out a scheme——"

Midge listened with half an ear to the girl who had promised to mind her own business: but without suggesting any schemes. It was the Gascoignes themselves who played into Susan's hands. Gabrielle came flying along to the Chalet du Lac after lunch.

"Oh will you and Susan do us a favour?" she said to Midge. "Meet Gina Prescott's boat and show her the hotel? Peregrine is so much better this afternoon and he's *dying* to go up the Burgenstock and Selina can't bear to disappoint him after his being so ill, poor sweet, and he wants us all to go. You weren't doing anything special, were you?"

"What time is she due to arrive?" asked Midge reluctantly. She wanted to tell Gabrielle to spoil her own afternoon and go and meet her own friends,

and the only reason she didn't was because Susan
was giving her such meaning looks.

"The boat that gets here about half-past three,"
said Gabrielle. "She's coming from Lucerne——"

"Right in the middle of the afternoon," muttered
Midge, but Susan gave her another meaning look and
Midge didn't say any more on that point. "How do
we recognise her?" she asked.

"Well to begin with," said Gabrielle, "she'll be the
smartest person on the boat. She's not very tall,
about Selina's height, and dark—you couldn't miss
her. Well, thanks a lot——!" and she was off to the
Burgenstock.

"You notice they don't ask us to go," said Bill, who
rather fancied the Burgenstock. "They must have
got some grander friends. They only ask us, it seems,
when nothing better turns up."

"Surely you don't want to go with the Ghastlys?"
Midge asked in blank amazement.

"No, of course not," said Bill. "Only I think it was
cheek not asking us."

"Yes, well never mind that now," said Susan, who
was looking excited. "D'you realise that we're going
to have this travel person in our clutches?"

"And what do you mean to do with her when
you get her in your clutches, you old vulture?" said
Midge.

"Oh, shut up, Midge," said Susan giggling. "Vulture, really!"

"Well, what *are* you going to do with her?"

"Kidnap her, of course!"

"Oh, of *course*——"

"You needn't put on that sarcastic voice," said Susan, "this is the luckiest thing that could have happened! We'll meet the boat, cook up some story about the Gascoignes' hotel and bring her to the Chalet du Lac! Then she'll write articles about how wonderful it is and people will flock to it and Herr and Frau Stocker will make their fortune!"

The only snag in this master plan was that when they went to see Frau Stocker she said that she was very sorry, but that she hadn't a room.

Susan wasn't too pleased. Really, Frau Stocker would have to be more co-operative than that. Here was Susan, going to all this trouble to get this travel person or whatever she was to come to the Chalet du Lac and all Frau Stocker could do was announce calmly that there wasn't a room! Susan explained again, more slowly and loudly, just how important this Miss Prescott was, but Frau Stocker seemed to be quite stupid about the whole thing and simply refused to push another guest out in the street to make room for her. Susan was in despair. Then suddenly she had a bright idea and said, "I know what! Let her have Charlotte's room! Charlotte can have my bed and I'll go in with Midge. After all, it's only for a night or two!"

Nobody was keen on this plan except Susan, but in her usual infectious way she convinced them that it was better than it sounded, then settled the matter by tossing half Charlotte's things out of her room before she could register any effective protests.

Everything went off quite according to plan. Miss Prescott was perfectly docile about being taken to another hotel; she exclaimed in delight at the beauties of the chalet and admired her bedroom and the view up the lake. There was an anxious moment before dinner when Susan on her way through the garden with Midge to the dining-room saw Peregrine lurking in the bushes.

"I say, what's Pea-green doing here?" she asked.

"Where is Pea-green?"

"Down there in the bushes——"

"Up to no good, I'll be bound," said Midge. "It's a pity he didn't fall down the Burgenstock."

"We don't want him to get talking to Miss Prescott at this stage," said Susan.

"We'd better send him off with a flea in his ear," said Midge.

However, when they ran down to the bushes, Peregrine hadn't waited to get a flea in his ear. There was no sign of him. "He must have seen us," said Susan. "We had better prowl round a bit and find him."

"Oh mercy, *no*," said Midge. "I don't feel in the *least* like crawling round the bushes. Look, there's Miss Going Places. Let's go and lead her into dinner and she'll think what polite girls we are and what nice people come to this hotel——"

Their plans went even better later because Miss Prescott was so exhausted with all her journeying (which didn't, in Susan's opinion, say much for either her stamina as a professional traveller or her travel arrangements) that she went to bed immediately after a most heavenly dinner. "So the Ghastlys can't drag her to their horrid hotel to-night at least," said Susan with great satisfaction, "whatever they may do to-morrow. We'd better amble along and tell them what we've done with Miss Prescott——" she added, not looking forward to this part of the programme quite so much.

By a stroke of luck the Gascoignes weren't in their hotel when the girls got there. "Gone off to guzzle cakes at the Confiserie Hofmann as usual I expect," said Midge. "Oh well, that suits us. We'll leave a note——"

They argued a bit about the wording of the note, but as Midge was the acknowledged literary member of the family, having actually had a story accepted for a book,* Susan was obliged to give way over this and Midge wrote, *Miss Prescott arrived safely. Had to go to another hotel. Will see you to-morrow, she says.*

" 'Had to go to another hotel' is good," said Susan in approval. "And by the time she sees the Ghastlys she'll be so pleased with the Chalet du Lac that she won't want to move——"

Unfortunately things didn't turn out as Susan had hoped. And really, she felt bound to admit afterwards, this time it was all her fault. At least the noise in the garden that wakened her in the middle of the night wasn't her fault—she didn't know whose fault that was. She didn't even know *what* it was. Later everybody decided that it must have been one of the Rosendorf cats having a good old night-howl; at the time it seemed like a child crying in terrible distress. Susan, of course, couldn't listen to such sounds of misery without wanting to do something about it; Midge,

* See *Susan Rushes In*

equally of course, refused to waken up however much
Susan prodded her, so there was nothing for it but
that Susan should get up and deal with the matter
on her own. When she got down to the garden there
was absolutely nothing out of the way to be found.
She stumbled about in the darkness for a bit, knocking
into trees and getting the bottoms of her pyjama
legs very wet on the dewy grass without finding the
cause of the distressing noises she had heard. However,
all this stumbling about and so on was of inconvenience
only to herself, it was what happened next that caused
the trouble. She went upstairs again, the chalet seem-
ing extra dark after the lesser darkness of the garden,
and into her room. She said afterwards that the room
felt jolly queer and that she kept bumping into hard
lumps that she wasn't expecting, but at the time she
just thought that the darkness was confusing her.
When she tried to get into bed she found that Midge
had rolled right to the front and proved very difficult
to dislodge. Susan tried to slide in carefully, but half
of herself was left hanging over the edge of the bed.
She tried pushing gently, but Midge would *not* budge.
"Oh bother you, Midge!" she exclaimed. If Midge
wouldn't move, there was nothing for it but to climb
over her. Susan started to clamber over the recumbent
figure. She put out her hand to steady herself. It was
a pity that her hand landed on Midge's face—what was
more of a pity was that it wasn't Midge's face at
all, for the recumbent figure groaned, gasped and a
voice quite different from Midge's shouted out, "Oh
this is *too* much!" and someone who certainly wasn't
Midge gave a great heave and sat up in bed and

snapped on the light, whereupon Susan's precarious hold on the bed was loosened and she fell flat on the floor.

Her horror when she looked up and saw the face of Miss Prescott glaring at her over the side of the bed was indescribable.

"This is too much!" Miss Prescott exclaimed again. "I find my bed stuffed with dead fish and wet sponges and when I get all that dealt with and get to sleep at *last* a lunatic girl comes barging into my bed, pushing my face in!"

Susan didn't know what she was talking about. All this rubbish about dead fish was so much nonsense to her, she thought that she wasn't hearing properly. She was in such a state of shame and embarrassment it wouldn't be surprising if she had gone dotty, far less deaf.

"I—I—I——" she began.

"Were *you* responsible for all those things?"

"All what things?" asked Susan in a small quavering voice.

"All those," said Miss Prescott, waving a furious hand at the floor.

Susan turned her head and looked. There was a large dead fish, a very spiky hairbrush, a long thorny briar from a climbing rose in the garden, an ash-tray with a lot of sharp corners, a book or two, a walking-stick with a nice metal point, a large wet sponge and a mouse-trap. Susan stared at them vacantly and then stared at Miss Prescott.

"All these things," said Miss Prescott, "were in my bed. Did you put them there?"

"Me?" said Susan, her voice a squeak. "Of course not!"

"You only put yourself, I suppose. For heaven's *sake* why were you clambering over me like an elephant in the middle of the night?"

There might have been occasions when Susan would have been rather offended at being compared to an elephant, but this wasn't one of them; she was too abject to take offence at anything. "Och, Miss Prescott," she burst out, "I'm *terribly* sorry! There was a noise in the garden you see and I got up to see what it was you see and when I came back I must have come into the wrong room by mistake. You see, my room is just next door and I'm sharing a bed with my cousin Midge because—well anyway I'm sharing a bed with her you see——"

Miss Prescott was obviously bored by this rambling and rather feeble explanation. "I see that I'm having a very uncomfortable night," she said. "It will perhaps teach me to remember to lock my door and not to visit hotels that I know nothing about——"

With these ominous words she dismissed Susan, who crept off to the half of Midge's bed in very low spirits.

Her spirits went even lower next morning after breakfast when she saw Hans the hotel boots putting Miss Prescott's very smart luggage into his trailer at the door of the chalet. Susan had recounted the night's misadventures to the rest of the family who had shrieked with laughter. They had decided that the apple-pie bed had been one of Peregrine's sweet little ideas—"So that was what he was up to, creeping about the garden!" said Midge—but of course no one could blame Susan's clambering over a strange lady in the middle of the night on anybody but Susan. Susan felt this acutely as she watched Miss Prescott's luggage going into the trailer. At that moment Miss Prescott came out of the chalet. Susan tried to hide behind a bush, but she had been seen.

"Good morning," said Miss Prescott.

"Good morning," whispered Susan. "Did you sleep—er——" She trailed off into silence, looking miserably at the luggage. "Does this mean that you're leaving, Miss Prescott?" she said in a very small voice.

"I'm leaving," Miss Prescott agreed. "I'm past the age for roughing it in second-rate hotels." Susan squirmed. "And while we're on the subject," Miss Prescott went on, "what was the idea in getting me here in the first place?" Susan looked at her. "You did get me here, you and those other girls, didn't you? There really wasn't any mistake about my booking at the Splendide, was there?"

"No," said Susan.

"But why? What was the idea?"

"Well——" said Susan. "Well," she rushed on, "it was because of you and *Going Places*. We thought our little Chalet du Lac was so sweet, much nicer than the Splendide; Frau Stocker has just started and we thought that if you came here and——" she gulped "—and liked it, you would say so in your articles and lots of English people would come and Frau Stocker would have a great success——"

"I see," said Miss Prescott in a slightly softer voice.

She added, "I should probably have come here later—at least for a meal—in any case, you know——"

"Oh," said Susan forlornly. Hans, the luggage loaded, mounted his bicycle and pedalled off. "Can I help you to carry anything, or anything?" said Susan.

"No thank you," said Miss Prescott, rather quickly, Susan thought. "Well, good-bye or should I say *au revoir* as I'll probably see you around with the Gascoignes——?"

Susan said yes, probably, dreading the thought of it; and Miss Prescott departed.

It was very small consolation when Frau Stocker told her after breakfast that the people to whom she had so kindly written were coming for three weeks.

"Oh, good," said Susan, "although," she added to Midge, "I'd be surprised if they didn't after what I said——"

"What did you say?"

"I put a P.S. and said ' I do think you ought to come because it's the most heavenly hotel in the most heavenly village '——"

"Honestly, Susie," said Charlotte, "you can't even write a letter for the hotel without interfering."

"Oh, but I've stopped," said Susan. "Stopped interfering. Midge is absolutely right. I'm never going to interfere again. I interfere with Lise and look what happens—I've only made her as mad as a snake and stuck her more firmly to that beastly sofa of hers than if I had glued her. And as for Miss Prescott and the hotel—well if I *hadn't* interfered, the Chalet du Lac would probably have got into Miss Prescott's articles——"

"Quite right," Midge agreed cheerfully. "As an interferer you'd better go out of business. Actually Susie, you'll find it's not so bad, minding your own business—peaceful, you know——"

One small but not to be despised consequence of the Prescott disaster was that the Carmichaels had a quiet day without the Gascoignes who were much too busy showing Miss Prescott the sights to join the others in an expedition. The expedition was to the Joch Pass, for Aunt Lucy and Uncle Charles and Bill refused to be put off any longer by the girls' lack of enthusiasm. And in the end it turned out to be a glorious excursion, one of the very best they had done. They started off, as they always did, by boat, then from Stansstad to a place called Engelberg took a mountain railway which ran up a beautiful valley along by a rushing jade-green river, through summer meadows and glorious beech-woods. Engelberg was a pleasant mountain village with nice shops, in one of which Susan bought a tiny carved wooden bear—she had been looking at bears in all shapes and sizes ever since coming to Switzerland and at last she had decided on one, the smallest she had seen, about the size of her thumb-nail, it was sweet. Then they walked along a little path through the fields to the next train, which was a funicular, then changed on to a real cable-railway with a nice big solid car which held at least forty people into which they were comfortably fastened by a guard who went with them, and it wasn't terrifying at all, not like that atrocity at Wissifluh, and Susan was able to look out of the window at the wonderful panorama of meadows and mountains and distant snow-peaks spreading out before them. The cable-railway took them to Trübsee. A hotel was perched on the very edge of space in a very dizzy and alarming manner but they walked quickly past that and came to the Trübsee itself, a most beautiful little lake with the mountains reflected in its still depths. Then came the chair-lift that would take them up to the Joch Pass and Susan's heart sank. She watched a few people get on—they took a flying leap at these ghastly chairs which kept going up and down the mountainside in a sort of perpetual motion. Then it was her turn. She made the leap quite successfully, helped by an attendant who clamped a safety bar down in front of her and pushed her off into space. After a little she opened her eyes and realised that this wasn't terrifying at all, but thrilling and delightful, like being a fairy or something, floating along in the air, not too far from the ground. She was even able to take her hands off the bar, which she had been gripping so fiercely that her hands were quite numb, and actually waved to Midge in the next chair which made her feel a positive dare-devil. She looked round at the scenery and could see the flowers on the mountain-side beneath her and the alpine roses, and some little furry animals, rather like beavers, she thought, scuttled away. Uncle Charles told them afterwards that they were marmots and Susan felt thankful that that dreadful Pea-green wasn't with them, taking pot shots at the marmots with his gun.

There was no road through the Joch Pass, it was

only a pass through the mountains, wild and lonely, with Titlis, which was the name of Bill's favourite boat on Lake Lucerne and which turned out to be a mountain, looming above them and the snow peaks gleaming beyond. There were great patches of snow still in the places where the sun didn't reach and the sweet, flat music of the cow bells in the air and flowers everywhere—in one little patch Charlotte found gentians and crocuses and soldanella, the fragile little fringed mauve bells which Susan thought were the daintiest of all the Alpine flowers although the gentians were still her favourite. It was heavenly to be right up there among the mountains—seven thousand two hundred and forty-five feet above sea level Bill told them—and *heavenly* to be there without the Gascoignes. . . .

When they returned to the Chalet du Lac that evening and went in to dinner, the first person they saw was Miss Prescott. Susan clutched Midge's arm and said that she thought she was going to faint. Midge said, "Don't be silly, she's grinning like the Cheshire Cat. She can't blame you for anything this time, besides, she looks as pleased as Punch——"

And such, oddly enough, appeared to be the case. Miss Prescott came across to their table after dinner and was introduced to Aunt Lucy and Uncle Charles by a very self-conscious Charlotte. But Miss Prescott had evidently forgiven them. She grinned conspiratorially at Susan. "I came back, you see," she said. "The Splendide was very *splendide* and grand—but my dear, the food was *terrible*! At least, what there was of it was all right, but so scanty! I had lunch there but that finished me, I was starving all afternoon! So I rushed back here as soon as I could—how thankful I was that Susan had introduced me to the Chalet du Lac!"

Aunt Lucy couldn't make out where Susan came into this story, but then that was often the way with Susan's appearances in unexpected places and situations, so she didn't go into the matter. Uncle Charles said what a shame that the Gascoignes' hotel was like that, and his children and niece all said *what* a shame in very false tones.

"So *that* explains why the Gascoignes were always stuffing themselves with cakes and chocolates!" exclaimed Midge. "I thought it was pure greed!"

"I'm jolly glad that their grand hotel isn't as good as ours after all," said Bill.

"Perhaps this will teach them not to treat us as if we were slumming," said Charlotte.

"Nothing teaches the Gascoignes," said Midge. "And nothing teaches Susan either," she added gloomily. "Just when I get her nice and humble and ready to renounce interference for ever, along comes this Miss Prescott business and it turns out that Susan has done some good at last with her interfering ways."

But Susan grinned and said that Midge needn't worry, that her failure with Lise would keep her humble for the rest of her life!

CHAPTER TEN

LOST!

AND NOW, unbelievably, it was the last day of their stay at Rosendorf. The Gascoignes were waiting a few days longer which was a great relief as Susan said, because a train and plane journey with Pea-green and a gun was more than her nerves could stand. Lise's father, Herr Schriber, had said good-bye a few days previously as he was returning to Zürich on business for a little while: he made a plan to meet them for lunch in Zürich on their way home. Fräulein Amacher called in to see them after breakfast, for Johann the chauffeur was driving her to Interlaken to see a sick friend. She gave presents to all the young people, carved by the man who kept the nicest shop in Rosendorf—a tiny cuckoo clock for Bill, a beautiful little carved foal, with stiff, braced legs and perky tail, for Susan, a grey kid with knobbly horns for Midge, a box for Charlotte to hold her trinkets which played a tune when you opened the lid. They were all quite stuttery with delight. But Fräulein Amacher waved away their thanks and said that they were doing a great kindness to her by taking the little boy back to London with them. She gave Uncle Charles the boy's ticket and passport.

After she had gone, Susan idly picked up the passport. It was in the name of Rudi Panacek—it was the passport from the pound of tea! Susan nearly fainted. She made signs to the others to come out into the garden where Uncle Charles and Aunt Lucy couldn't hear. She was breathless with excitement when she told the others.

"Rudi Pancake! The boy in the pound of tea, I mean the boy whose tea was in the passport, I mean— well anyway the boy we're taking to England is Rudi Pancake!"

"Gosh!" said Bill. "The famous scientist's son!"

Midge and Charlotte were speechless.

"Rudi Pancake!" said Susan in an awed voice when she had recovered her breath. "I just simply never connected him with the boy we were taking to England, did you?"

None of them had had any such idea in their heads. They were all as amazed as Susan.

"Little did we think," she said, her eyes gleaming, "that *we* would be the ones to smuggle him into England!"

Charlotte suddenly looked nervous. She could picture Susan carrying on in so conspiratorial a manner that a half-wit with poor eyesight would know that there was something suspicious going on, far less an alert customs-officer.

Susan indignantly denied this. She would behave so naturally, she said, that the customs people would think that Rudi was her little brother, or cousin, or something.

"Gosh," said Bill, "poor kid!"

It had been arranged that they would collect Rudi at the See Perle, and that he would spend the night at the Chalet du Lac, for the party were catching a very early boat so that they could spend a little time in Zürich before getting their plane to London. They all went to the See Perle in the morning to meet Rudi. Then they had a last swim and a last walk round the high meadows above the village and a last prowl round the shops and a last caféglacé as a last treat at the Confiserie Hofmann, and it seemed to them that Rosendorf looked gayer and prettier than ever, with tempting posters of future attractions—fireworks in Lucerne that very night and a display of flag-throwing, which was a very clever thing the Swiss did with flags, and Alphorn blowing the following Sunday. "Funny," said Susan, "all these arrangements! I never can believe that things still go on when I leave a place, I just imagine everything stopping when I'm not there."

Everybody agreed that they all felt like that, and Midge said, "Imagine everybody having fun in Rosendorf and us at home in boring old London! It makes going away much worse."

"In fact," said Susan, "smuggling Rudi through the customs and immigration and so on will be the only bright spot in a very gloomy future——"

After dinner, while Aunt Lucy was doing some last-minute packing with Uncle Charles rather reluctantly in attendance to sit on the cases and strap them up, Susan and the Carmichaels walked along to the See Perle to say good-bye to Lise and collect Rudi. Nobody noticed two small boys crouched behind the bushes that grew between the road and the lake, or saw two pairs of eyes peering at them as they passed.

They said good-bye to Lise, and Susan nobly restrained herself from any last exhortations to get on her feet, and they all said that they would write to Lise, even Bill, and Lise promised to come and see them when next she came to London with her father; and at last Charlotte said reluctantly, "Well, I suppose we must go or Aunt Lucy will be getting in a flap. Where's Rudi, is he ready?"

Lise looked blank. "But Rudi's with you!" she said.

Susan and the Carmichaels looked blanker. "But of course he's not with us!" said Charlotte. "We came to fetch him!"

"But Peregrine came to fetch him!" Lise exclaimed. "Just before you came! You must have met them on the road!"

"We met nobody," said Charlotte, "and why should Pea-green come to fetch him?"

"I do not know!" said Lise helplessly. "He said that you had asked him to come for Rudi!"

"That Pea-green!" Charlotte exclaimed. "One of these days I really will wring his neck! And now we'll have to traipse along to the Splendide to collect Rudi!"

"I shall telephone," said Lise and she picked up the telephone that was always placed on a little table beside her sofa when she was indoors in the drawing-room. She spoke in Swiss, and then in a minute or two she said, "Good evening, Adrian—yes, very well, thank you . . . oh, thank you. . . . We are wondering if Rudi is there, he is with Peregrine just a little while ago . . . oh! . . . Oh? . . . Oh, I see . . . well, thank you Adrian . . . yes, I will tell you . . . good-bye." She put down the receiver and turned to the others looking puzzled. "Adrian does not know anything about Rudi," she said. "Peregrine has gone to Lucerne to see the fireworks with a guest in the hotel—they have just left to catch the boat——"

Charlotte said, "Tt! What a muddle! D'you imagine that they've taken Rudi too?"

Susan said, "Who has taken Pea-green to Lucerne, did Adrian say?"

"Yes," said Lise, "a Herr Gruber or some such——" she stopped abruptly and stared for Susan had bounded to her feet with such energy that she had sent her chair flying.

"Lise!" gasped Susan. "There's something wrong!" Then she paused. An icy hand seemed to have closed round her heart—something was wrong, she knew it— why *should* Pea-green come for Rudi whom he had met for the first time that day unless—unless Herr Gruber had told him to? And yet how was she going to say anything about Herr Gruber without also telling of the way she had been poking her nose into everybody's business? Really, what *could* she say?

The others were all talking at once.

"*Hon*estly, Susie, why should anything be wrong?"

"Susan, remember ducky, no interfering——"

"You'll call *wolf, wolf* once too often——"

But Susan had made up her mind. "Be quiet a minute, all of you," she said. "Lise, hadn't you better tell us? There *is* some mystery about Rudi, isn't there?"

Lise went red. "No, naturally not," she said, "why should there be?"

"Because there's a mystery about Herr Gruber!"

cried Susan. "He tried to push me under a car in the Kapellgasse and on the pretence of pulling me back he tried to grab Fräulein Amacher's pound of tea, and the next thing we knew he had turned up here in Rosendorf and made friends with the Gascoignes! And Lise," Susan added, going red in her turn, "we know what was in the pound of tea because we—at least, I—looked! And we saw the cutting about Rudi that fell out of your book the day you threw it at me——"

Lise had pushed herself bolt upright against the arms of her chair, and was staring at Susan. "We must find Rudi!" she said. "I do not *think* there can be anything wrong—but if it is true what you say —then, then there *is* something wrong—and I think— he may be in danger——"

That was enough for Susan. "We'll go after them!" she cried and all the Carmichaels got to their feet.

"There's an extra boat, specially for the fireworks, at half-past eight," said Bill. "Have we time——?"

At that moment there came the hoot that the little steamers gave as they approached Rosendorf. Susan and her cousins ran to the window. Curving in towards the pier, festooned with gay fairy-lights and flags, was the steamer.

"Run!" cried Susan and darted to the door.

"Oh Susan don't be dotty," said Midge, "we're half a mile from the pier, we'd never make it——"

"It's the only boat!" said Bill.

"When will Fräulein Amacher be back with your father's car?" asked Charlotte.

"Not till late! Not till ten o'clock, I am sure!"

"What are we to *do*?" cried Susan. "There's something wrong, I *know* there is! We *must* get to Lucerne, we must find Rudi! How can we get to Lucerne? We must get to Lucerne! Is there nobody——"

She stopped abruptly. She stared across the room at Lise and Lise stared back at her. And so, for a second, there was absolute silence in the room as Susan and Lise stared at each other and the others stood by, holding their breath. Then suddenly Lise twitched the silk shawl off her knees and swung her feet to the ground. "I'll take you," she said and stood up.

"Oh, *Lise*, good for you!" yelled Susan.

"Come!" said Lise and hobbled out of the room.

CHAPTER ELEVEN

THE SEARCH FOR RUDI

THEY RAN to the garage. "You don't . . . waddle . . . like a duck . . . at all!" panted Susan as they ran.

"It is more bad . . . when I am walking," Lise answered.

"Just keep . . . running, then," said Susan and everybody laughed and felt a little better. Lise wrenched open the garage doors. Lise's maid, with a look of stupefaction on her face, looked out of the kitchen door. Lise called to her in Swiss to tell the Herr Doktor at the Chalet du Lac that his family had gone out for a little and would be back soon, and they all piled into Lise's little car, specially designed that she could drive it without using her lame leg. They rushed through the summer night, on the upper road through Rosendorf away from the strolling holiday crowds, through Küssnacht, past the chapel on the spot where the Queen of the Belgians had been killed, through Meggen, round the arm of the lake towards Lucerne and as they went Lise told them about Rudi.

It was all pretty much as Susan had worked it out. Although Fräulein Amacher had not done the actual smuggling of Rudi into Switzerland, she had certainly arranged the smuggling of him into England. Rudi's father was a Czech, his name was Panacek, his mother had been Swiss and a pupil of Fräulein Amacher's,

168

but she had died some years previously. They had lived in Prague, behind the Iron Curtain of course, and Rudi's father had been forced to work for the communists—he was a very famous scientist, a nuclear physicist ("What's that?" asked Susan. "It's somebody who knows all about atom bombs," said Bill. "Do dry up, Susie——") and he had hated the communists. At last he managed to escape to England, but he had to leave his son behind. The communists had threatened to do dreadful things to the little boy unless Herr Panacek returned to Prague, but a few weeks before, Fräulein Amacher had had a letter from Rudi's father to say that friends were planning to get Rudi across Europe to Switzerland, could Fräulein Amacher get him to England?

"But surely," said Bill, "we, the British, I mean, would have let Rudi into England? England has always given—what's the word? Something to do with loonies——?"

"Asylum?" suggested Charlotte. "It means refuge, in this case——"

"Yes, asylum, asylum to refugees?"

"It was not that which worried Fräulein Amacher," said Lise, "it was that unless she was very secret about the whole affair the communists might track Rudi down and try to get him back—he was important to them as a hostage, they would try to force his father to return by threatening his life." There was a horrid little silence in the car, then Lise went on with the story. When Rudi arrived in Switzerland, Fräulein Amacher had sent him to a friend of hers at Wissifluh, to be safely out of the way——

"Why?" asked Bill. "I can't see the point in that——"

"Because," said Lise, "as soon as Rudi arrived in Switzerland Fräulein Amacher felt all the time that she was being watched. Her letters seemed to be tampered with—and that was why she had you bring out the tea, with Rudi's papers hidden in it——" Lise sounded embarrassed.

The air in the car was thick with the *I told you so's* that Susan was nobly managing not to say.

"So Susan was right from the very beginning," said Bill, "there *was* something queer about Fräulein Amacher's pound of tea!"

"But Lise," said Midge. "Why didn't Fräulein Amacher just tell us? *We* would have brought Rudi's papers——"

"Yes," said Lise, "we know now that you would, but then we did not know you. I—I am sorry about the smuggling——!"

"Och jings," said Susan, "don't be sorry! Nothing as exciting as this has ever happened to us before! But Lise, I asked Frau Weber up at Wissifluh if she knew Fräulein Amacher, and she said no——!"

"Well," said Lise, "did you imagine she would say anything else? To her you are a stranger—you might have been a communist spy!"

"Me?" said Susan, rather pleased. It sounded very exciting and dramatic. Then she said, "But Frau Tannenbaum, the neighbour! She was the spy, wasn't she? She was spying all the time——"

"Yes, after what you told Fräulein Amacher, she is sure that it was Frau Tannenbaum. At the time she did not think of Frau Tannenbaum, but in any case she decided not to take Rudi to England herself as she had planned to do, that was too dangerous for Rudi, she thought, she decided to smuggle him away with the help of some English people. Rudi's father was somehow to obtain a passport or an entry permit, which he did and sent in the tea, with a letter and some money for Frau Weber, because by this time Fräulein Amacher was afraid to trust to the post. And she liked the sound of you when your aunt wrote for rooms——" (the Carmichaels and Susan smirked a little in the darkness) "—and among so many children Rudi, she thought, would not be noticed. She did not tell the Herr Doktor and Fräulein Carmichael anything about it—perhaps it was wrong, what she did, but she thought it was better, so that they would not feel uncomfortable being asked to do something against the law—and then too it was better that they know nothing if the officials at the airport start to ask the questions."

Susan waved aside all that bit about the law—it was a privilege, she considered, to be asked to do such an exciting thing. She said "And Herr Gruber? What about him, the beast? He tried to push me under a car——"

"I do not know anything about him," said Lise, "except that he and the neighbour must be together in this. I think from what you say that he tried to get the parcel because he guessed it was important, perhaps he even guessed that it had Rudi's papers in it; when he did not succeed in that he decided perhaps to follow you until you should lead him to Rudi. He did not know how much you realised of what he had done in the Kapellgasse so he does not risk trying to be friendly with you, he becomes instead friendly with the Gascoignes——"

"And probably got all the information he needed out of Pea-green——"

"And used Pea-green to entice Rudi away with this tale about fireworks——"

"I should *never* have let Rudi go with Peregrine," said Lise. "But I did not think it any harm—I thought everything was safe—it has all been my fault——"

Nonsense, the Carmichaels said. Besides, it was too late to worry about that. The important thing *now* was, what was the next step, what was the best thing to do?

"If we get to the quay before the boat arrives then everything will be all right," said Bill. "We grab Rudi, give Pea-green a punch on the nose, push Herr Gruber into the lake and go home." Midge and Susan cheered loudly.

"Yes, it will be all right if we reach the quay before the boat," said Lise more soberly, and accelerated.

"Lise, if we don't reach the quay in time," said Bill, "where will this man take Rudi?"

"I do not know where he will take him at first," said Lise. "Afterwards, I know, he will take him to Prague—and that will be the end of our plans—perhaps even of Rudi——"

There was silence. Everybody felt slightly sick. The headlights cut a path in the darkness ahead as the car rushed on, and picked out chalets and trees and gardens and sometimes a distant glimmer of the lake.

Not far to go now—they were approaching the outskirts of Lucerne.

Susan said in a diffident voice, "Don't you think that Grub or whatever his name is might take Rudi to Frau Tannenbaum's flat? After all, they're in league or we think they are——"

"We had better split up," said Bill, "two can go straight to the flat in the Kornmarkt and the rest go to the quay——"

"I'll go to the Kornmarkt," offered Midge. She didn't fancy snatching Rudi out of the clutches of Herr Gruber in full view of half of Lucerne.

Susan didn't in the least want to go to the flat. That old, old house—and that horrible Frau Tannenbaum who watched people through a crack in the door —Susan was terrified at the thought of Frau Tannenbaum. But on the other hand Charlotte and Lise, who were practically grown-up, would be the best ones to confront that Gruber—and Bill would be useful in case there was any fighting. "I'll go to the flat with Midge," she said in a quavering voice.

Lise said, "I think that there will be no need. I think we will be in time——"

But she had reckoned without the crowds. Lucerne was *en fête* that night. To reach the quays Lise had to cross the main bridge, the Seebrücke, that spanned the river Reuss where it left the lake and went from the Schwanenplatz, behind which stretched the old town, to the station. Crowds lined the bridge and jostled happily on the pavements; cars were in a solid mass.

"Oh," cried Lise, "this is hopeless!"

"There's a boat approaching the quay now! Is that the Rosendorf boat?" cried Bill.

"Hadn't we better get out and run?" said Charlotte. "Come on, Bill!"

"Yes, yes," said Lise. "I will park the car where I can. All meet at the *Schwanen*—you know it?—the big cafe at the corner of the Schwanenplatz—go now!"

Charlotte and Bill jumped out, crossed the road with some difficulty and began to dodge along the crowded pavement. Midge and Susan got out too. They hurried through the strolling crowds to the Kapellplatz which led to the Kapellgasse, and as they did so the first fireworks burst in a blaze of colour and light, a dazzle of whirls and stars and cascades and drops of coloured fire. The crowd sighed, " O-o-o-oh! A-a-a-ah!" their upturned faces brilliantly lit for a second by red and blue and unearthly green.

Ever afterwards Susan was to think of that weird and terrifying night in Lucerne whenever she watched fireworks. The Kapellgasse was quiet and empty; their footsteps rang out in the deserted Kornmarkt —everyone had hurried to the lake-side or the bridges to watch the fireworks. The two girls went to the old house where Fräulein Amacher lived, and stood by the dark doorway.

No one stirred in the silent Corn Market; even in the windows there seemed to be no lights, no sign of life. Every now and then sprays of fiery stars shot into the night sky and lit up the old shuttered houses, the ancient crooked gables, the blind windows. The girls could hear the crack and bang of the fireworks and the distant murmur of the crowds.

"I wish——" Susan began and stopped because her voice had come out in a frightened squeak. She tried again. "I wish something would happen," she said more firmly.

"Not me," said Midge. "Quite enough is happening for my taste."

"I hate just standing here, waiting," whispered Susan.

"Shall one of us go to the Swan and see if Rudi has been found?" said Midge.

"Which one?" quavered Susan.

"You, if you like," said Midge, after a pause. "You know I hate walking."

Susan was tempted. To be *doing* something—even if it was only running to the *Schwanen*—! Then she said, "I can't leave you here, all alone."

"Yes you can," said Midge. "I'll whistle hymns all the time to keep the bogie-man away like we did when we were kids——"

"All right," said Susan. "I'll run all the way——" and she was gone.

There was no one at the *Schwanen*—not Lise nor Charlotte nor Bill that is, although, Susan thought, there were about ten million other people. She pushed her way in and out of the crowds, peering and looking for the others. The café was crowded, crowds thronged the pavement outside and crowds sat at the tables eating ices and drinking coffee and bright-coloured drinks in tall glasses. It was gay and noisy and happy and normal and Susan hated to leave it, hated to leave the people and go back to the dark emptiness of the Kornmarkt. But that thought reminded her of Midge, and she pushed her way through the crowds towards the Kapellgasse.

It was then that she saw them. A brilliant flare of livid green shot up, the crowd parted for a moment and she saw them—Herr Gruber's unmistakable flaxen head, Rudi's thin little dark face and Peregrine's handsome black curls. Under her breath she exclaimed in joy and relief and began pushing towards them.

This wasn't a popular move at all. The crowd was thick just there, where the bridge joined the Schwanenplatz, and no one saw any reason for allowing Susan to push her way to a better position. Susan was in despair. If she could only reach them! If she could only get through! They would move, she would lose them—and all these people glaring at her and muttering! She was nearly crying with worry and disappointment and frustration when she finally came up against an immovable back, a back that was apparently determined to budge for no one. "Oh, please, *please* let me through!" Susan almost sobbed. The back turned and she was gazing into the face of the cross little schoolmaster who had slapped her when they were at Rigi Kulm, his bevy of twelve or so little boys clustered round him.

He recognised her too, and gave his little stiff unsmiling bow. "Fräulein," he said.

"Oh, I'm *sorry* if I pushed you," Susan cried, "but I'm in terrible trouble, Mr.—er—Monsieur—er—Herr Professor!"

The little schoolmaster, pleased perhaps by his elevation to professorial rank, looked sympathetic and alarmed. "What is it, Fräulein? What is happen?"

"Herr Professor," said Susan, pleased too that she had finally found some way of addressing him, "we have lost two little boys and I saw them a minute ago in the crowd, and now I can't get through to them——"

"Fraulein," said the Herr Professor, "be not longer unquiet. My boys and I will help you to uncover them. Describe the lost boys——!"

"Oh, *thank* you, Herr Professor!" cried Susan. "One is a very handsome little boy with black curly hair, he's wearing the most terrible clothes, dungarees and a very loud shirt——" she saw the Herr Professor open his mouth to ask how a shirt could be loud and hurried on as she didn't feel capable of explaining, "he's nine. And the other is the same age, but much smaller, and very thin, rather plain really, and he's not so smart either, he's wearing grey trousers that are too long for him and a lumber jacket. One of the boys," she added, "the handsome one, has a gun."

The Herr Professor looked absolutely astonished. He did not waste time asking questions however, he rapidly translated for the benefit of his boys, who every now and then stopped listening to gaze skyward at some startling burst of fire; then he barked out a few orders and the boys grinned, told Susan that they would all re-assemble here at the *Schwanen* in half an hour and all twelve of them began to slip and slide away and worm through the crowd like Red Indians.

Even if they didn't do any good, Susan thought, they were so kind that she felt better. She looked round about her again and craned her neck in all directions but she couldn't see the two boys and Herr

Gruber anywhere. She felt that they must have moved—but how was she to know in which direction? She didn't know what to do. She hated to leave the spot where she had seen Rudi, but on the other hand she ought to get back to Midge, who would be wondering what had happened to her—— She edged out of the crowd and slipped into the quietness of the Kapellgasse. . . .

Midge leant up against the wall of the old house and looked across the dark square. She might, she thought fancifully, have been the only person left alive in a town of the dead, and she wished that old Susan would come thumping back and waken up these black shadows which seemed to lurk in the corners. She felt depressed—how could they ever hope to find Rudi in this old town, full of twisting streets, full too of gay holiday crowds watching fireworks? As for Pea-green, well, she thought, she didn't much care if she never did find him, that fugitive from a horror-comic, that ghastly little assistant-kidnapper. Although, she added to herself, to do him justice he probably had no idea that he was assisting in a kidnapping—nasty Herr Gruber had probably told him a fine convincing tale.

At that precise point in her meditations, a flash of light across the sky lit up the little square and she saw the object of her thoughts standing hesitating at the corner of the Kapellgasse, his awful gun under one arm. "*Pea-green!*" she shouted and ran across the square to him. She caught him by the arm. "Pea-green," she said, "where's Rudi?"

Peregrine disengaged his arm with dignity. "*I* don't know where that boring child is," he said in his high prim voice. "In fact, if you ask me, I think this whole expedition has been a trifle boring. 'Come to Lucerne and see the fireworks,' Herr Gruber said. 'Get Rudi to come,' he said, 'it will be fun for him seeing he's going to England to-morrow. Don't tell these Carmichaels or we shall have to ask——' "

"How did he know about Rudi?" Midge interrupted.

"*I* don't know," said Peregrine impatiently. "I suppose I told him. He asked me plenty of questions about Rudi—where is he now, who's taking him to England, when are your friends—that's you—going to England—I got very bored with it, I can tell you. And then when we got here," he went on broodingly, "Herr Gruber wanted us to go and see his boring old sister or cousin or somebody. Said she would give us cakes and hot chocolate. That was all very well, I thought, for I was hungry, and I should have liked some cakes later, but after all we *had* come to see the fireworks. So I put my foot down. 'We'll look at the fireworks first,' I said, 'and then we'll be delighted to have cakes and chocolate with your grandmother——' "

"And then?" Midge prompted. If only the little beast would tell her where Rudi was *now*! It worried her sick that Herr Gruber now had Rudi by himself, without even Pea-green's doubtful support——

"And then?" said Peregrine. "Well, *then* was what made me very cross, I can tell you—we were standing watching the fireworks—not bad, didn't you think?— when I happened to glance round and there was Herr

Gruber edging Rudi out of the crowd—sneaking off to have cakes and chocolate without me! I edged after them pretty smartly, I can tell you, but the crowd was rather thick there and I lost them. I thought they slipped into this little street but——"

There was a scurry of footsteps and Susan came into the Kornmarkt from the Kapellgasse. "Oh gosh, Midge! There you are!" she cried. "Anything been happening—*Pea-green!* Where did you come from? And where's Rudi?"

"I wish people wouldn't keep on asking me where Rudi is," said Peregrine in a displeased voice. "I don't know where Rudi is——"

"I know where Rudi is!" interrupted Midge. She pointed to the opposite corner of the square. "There he is!"

"Rudi!" yelled Susan. "We're here! Hold on! We're coming!" She started to run across the square, Midge and Peregrine at her heels.

Herr Gruber, his flaxen hair white in the dim light, had Rudi firmly by the hand. He hesitated for a second, then he doubled back the way he had come, pulling the boy with him. Rudi dragged back with all his strength, glancing back imploringly over his shoulder. "Hold on, Rudi, we're coming!" Susan yelled again. But the little boy was so thin and light—Herr Gruber lifted him up and threw him over his shoulder like a sack of potatoes, and while Rudi beat with ineffectual fists against his back he disappeared down a dark and narrow street. . . .

When Lise had found a parking-place for her car

she went to the police headquarters. The police were very soothing, and told her that lost little boys always turn up.

Not if they're being kidnapped, Lise thought to herself, but she didn't say it aloud because she did not want to start explaining that one to the police. "We'll look out for him, Fräulein Schriber, don't worry," the police said and Lise went away. It was a slim chance, she felt, and she was afraid that it wouldn't be any good—but a policeman might just chance to see Rudi.

She made her way back to the *Schwanen* through the crowds, the fireworks bursting and glowing and showering coloured stars across the sky. That's what I feel like to-night, she thought, bursting and glowing with joy because I'm here, in Lucerne, on my own two legs again even if one is a bit dilapidated! I could shout and sing and dance with joy that I've come to my senses at last. And then, in between, everything is dark again when I think about Rudi and what may be happening to him at this very moment. Already he may be in a car—and she thought of dark and sinister people racing for the frontier and Rudi, helpless, with them. She shuddered, and slipped through the crowds. . . .

When Charlotte and Bill had struggled through the crowds and reached the quay to find an empty boat and the passengers dispersed, they looked at each other in despair.

"Now what?" said Bill.

"Heavens, Bill, I don't *know*," said Charlotte. "It's

worse, much worse I'd say, than looking for a needle in a haystack to look for one small boy in this mob——"

"Two small boys," said Bill.

"Don't alarm yourself, I'm not looking for Pea-green," she said grimly. "Unless with a view to murdering him. *Look* at the crowds!" She waved a hand towards the Seebrücke.

Bill brought his gaze down from the heavens, where it had been following an immense rocket which burst in a fountain of red and green stars. "'Mm," he said. "It's hopeless. But we must try. Would it be any good if we looked on this side of the river? That Gruber just *might* have taken this way——"

"I'm sure he'll make for that flat eventually," said Charlotte, "if he is in the plot with Frau Tannenbaum. And if he isn't, if this is just another figment of Susan's imagination, then he'll turn up at the Splendide safe and sound with the two boys and no one will be better pleased than I will—*we'll* look pretty silly, but I don't care, I'll look like a hysterical fool with the greatest of pleasure——"

"Gosh, I hope they do turn up," said Bill. "I hope it's all a mistake. It makes me feel very queer inside to think of that funny little boy being dragged back to Prague as a—what's the word?—a hostage? What will they do to him, d'you think, to persuade his father to go back?"

"I don't know," said Charlotte shortly. "Don't talk about it. Let's go——"

Bill said slowly, trying to think back to the sunny, carefree day when they had explored the town, "Now if we go along the river on this bank and cross that second old funny wooden bridge, which was called the Spreuerbrücke, I think, we come to the Mühlenplatz——"

"Where we had lunch one day, in that sweet little restaurant——"

"That's right," said Bill. "And that should lead us to the Wine Market and then to the Corn Market where Fräulein Amacher's house is and we can link up with Midge and Susan——"

"Come on then," said Charlotte, "let's do that."

They hurried along the embankment, and the fireworks lit up in flashes the swiftly running river and the upturned faces of the crowd, and the pens where the pampered ducks and swans lived and the ancient fronts of the houses opposite. The crowd thinned as they hurried along. A group of schoolboys, about six of them, Bill's age, came clattering over the footbridge and stood indecisively, chattering shrilly and obviously arguing. Charlotte and Bill hurried on. They came to the ancient wooden bridge and ran up the steps. . . .

Susan and Midge and Peregrine darted down the narrow street after Herr Gruber. He could run jolly fast, Susan thought, but it couldn't be easy running with a small boy slung across your shoulder, a small boy who was hammering on your back with his fists as hard as he could. At the bottom of the street Herr Gruber disappeared. His pursuers reached it only seconds after him. They hesitated a moment—left or right?—then Rudi called out and the sound came from the right. Another narrow street—which opened

out into another little square. They were too far from
the fireworks here for their light to be any help. They
could hear the distant bangs and behind them and
above the rockets still burst in showers of red and
green and gold. "I think . . this is . . . the Mühlenplatz," Susan panted. "Over there . . we had lunch
. . . that day. . . . Where d'you think he's . . . .
making for?"

"Don't know . . . just don't lose . . . sight of
him," Midge panted back.

"What are we all . . . running for?" panted Peregrine in an aggrieved voice, but nobody bothered
to answer him.

Suddenly Susan cried, "He's gone! I can't see him!"

They paused for a second, and heard the hollow
sound of footsteps ringing on wood.

"Bridge!" said Susan.

It was dark under the covered bridge, only lit by
the distant glow and flash of the fireworks. As a soar-
ing rocket gave a fitful light they saw Herr Gruber
heave the boy off his shoulder and try to drag him
along the bridge, Rudi resisting every inch. Susan
suddenly remembered what Peregrine was carrying.
She grabbed it from him and yelled, "Stop, Herr
Gruber! I have a gun!" and the old wooden roof
of the bridge threw back her voice eerily.

Charlotte and Bill, at the other end of the bridge,
heard the sound. "*Susan!*" they called and ran towards
her. They came face to face with Herr Gruber, dragging Rudi unmercifully by the arm. He, finding his
way barred, turned and rushed at Susan.

"Stop!" she cried. "I'll—I'll shoot!"

But Herr Gruber knew all about Peregrine's gun. He charged straight at Susan, grabbed the gun out of her hand and threw it down. Slinging Rudi under one arm he doubled back, slipped between Charlotte and Bill, taken by surprise.

"He'll get away! He'll get away!" cried Susan.

Suddenly there was the rush and thump of heavy boots as six bullet-headed little boys clattered along the bridge. Herr Gruber was in the midst of them, trying to barge his way through. "Stop him ! Stop him!" yelled Susan. "Stop that man! Stop him!" Charlotte and Bill turned and snatched Rudi out of his grasp. Herr Gruber was pushed and jostled in the cluster of little boys. He struck wildly at their faces and burst through their restraining hands. The sound of his frantic footsteps died away.

Charlotte gently took Rudi's hand and smiled at him. Rudi smiled back uncertainly. Susan grinned at the small boys led, she noticed, by Hansli and Anton, and felt like bursting into tears.

"Oh what *is* all this about?" said Peregrine crossly.

"Be *quiet*, Pea-green," said Susan. "It's all your fault!"

"Oh dry up and blow away!" said Peregrine. He picked up his gun and marched off. "Let's go back and look at the fireworks," he said.

CHAPTER TWELVE

Auf Wiedersehen!

THEY ALL met, at last, at the *Schwanen* and Lise hugged Rudi so hard that he squeaked and Susan, helped by Lise, made a polite speech to the Herr Professor, who bowed, and Anton and Hansli whispered to Susan that he, jerking their heads towards their teacher, was a very nice man now, never hit zem on ze ears, only on ze legs with a beeg steeck.

"Not Susan's interference at work *again*, surely," muttered Midge, but she hugged Susan with one arm as she spoke and said, "Good old Susie!"

Then the other contingent of the Herr Professor's pupils appeared. They had three small boys, who were sobbing bitterly, in tow whom they had torn away from their mothers by main force and who did not resemble Peregrine or Rudi in the slightest degree. The Herr Professor took one scandalised look at them. "Wrong boys," he barked. "Return them!"

Then they all said *auf wiedersehen*, which, Susan kindly told Bill who knew it already, meant *au revoir*, till we meet again, and the Herr Professor gathered his boys and departed and the others went to the car, dragging a reluctant Peregrine with them.

In the car going back to Rosendorf they talked and argued about what was to be told to Aunt Lucy and Uncle Charles. Nothing, said Lise. Everything, said the others. "But if we tell them everything and then Herr Doktor Carmichael finds that his conscience will not allow him to smuggle Rudi into England?" asked Lise.

The Carmichaels were quite insulted. How *could* Lise think of such dreadful things to say against their father who, to hear them talking, was the most reckless law-breaker in England?

"Besides," said Susan, her eyes gleaming at the idea, " supposing Frau Tannenbaum and Herr Gruber make another attack on the way home? If Aunt Lucy and Uncle Charles weren't warned they might let Rudi slip through sheer ignorance!" That seemed to settle it.

They handed Peregrine over to his doting mother and had much pleasure in telling her that her darling boy had just been rescued from a sort of kidnapper— not that anyone wanted to kidnap Pea-green, sorry, Peregrine, it was Rudi whom the kidnapper was after —Pea-green, sorry, Peregrine, was only a minor accomplice, but that they hadn't time to stop and explain then. "And I hope *that* thought gives her pleasant dreams!" said Susan.

They found Aunt Lucy up, as Bill said, to high doh, Uncle Charles threatening to send her to bed with two Aspirin, and Fräulein Amacher quite in the dark about what had happened and not daring to show her desperate anxiety, all together at the See Perle. The hilarious band of rescuers burst in, Aunt Lucy tried to scold them, Fräulein Amacher tried to embrace Rudi who was much too exhilarated by his recent adventures to put up with that sort of thing, and Uncle Charles was giving a slight rendering of a justifiably irate parent when Fräulein Amacher came to her senses, gasped and exclaimed, "Lise! You are walking!"

And Lise laughed and hugged her and said, "Yes, darling Fräulein, I have come to my senses at last!"

And Fräulein Amacher hugged *her*. "So!" she cried. "At last you have listened to the advice of your old Fräulein!"

And Lise laughed again and glanced at Susan, who was beaming proudly at this happy scene, and she said, "Well, truth to tell, dearest Fräulein Amacher, it was to Susan's advice that I listened!"

And the very last scene of this adventurous holiday? It took place at London Airport when, safely through the customs, all formalities over, Rudi rushed into the arms of a little dark-haired man, whose eyes were no longer sad and anxious.